"Listen, I really [text obscured] **forward. I wan**[text obscured] **to know you, co**[text obscured] **stuff…but right** [text obscured] **you to step into the office and close the door."**

Her eyes widened as she hesitated slightly before moving into the office slowly.

He followed her lead and closed the door behind them. Then, leaning forward, he covered her lips with his own.

Her mouth opened and she sighed. Her sweet mouth felt warm and welcoming. It had the taste of sweet cotton candy hot and fresh from Coney Island. He groaned inwardly, letting his tongue forge deeply into her mouth, twisting and turning, charting its path.

He lifted his arms and let his hands trail her body. She felt so good. Finally he pulled away and took a deep breath. The strong scent of honey, hibiscus and sweet desire assaulted his nostrils.

And then, with everything he had inside of him, he pulled away. Breathing came at great cost because every ounce of the air was laced with her. He couldn't stop now. He needed more. He needed her.

Books by Gwyneth Bolton

Kimani Romance

If Only You Knew
Protect and Serve
Make It Hot
The Law of Desire
Sizzling Seduction
Make It Last Forever

GWYNETH BOLTON

was born and raised in Paterson, New Jersey. She currently lives in Central New York with her husband, Cedric. When she was twelve years old, she became an avid reader of romance by sneaking books from her mother's stash of Harlequin and Silhouette novels. In the '90s she was introduced to African-American and multicultural romance novels and her life hasn't been the same since. She has a BA and MA in English/Creative Writing and a PhD in English/Composition and Rhetoric. She teaches classes in writing and women's studies at the college level. She has won several awards for her romance novels, including five Emma Awards and the Romance in Color Reviewers' Choice award for new author of the year.

When Gwyneth is not teaching or working on her own romance novels, she is curled up with a cup of herbal tea, a warm quilt and a good book. She can be reached via e-mail at gwynethbolton@prodigy.net. And readers can visit her Web site at www.gwynethbolton.com.

Make It
Last
FOREVER

GWYNETH BOLTON

KIMANI
ROMAN

This novel is dedicated to the editors because they make it
possible for us writers to make it do what it do!

To Angelique Justin for taking a chance on a new author and
publishing my very first novel

To Mavis Allen for believing that I—with my little one book
sold to another publisher—had a story strong enough to be one
of the launch books for Kimani Romance

And to Kelli Martin for helping me to continue honing my craft
and write better books each and every time and for making
"revision hell" a little less hellish…

KIMANI PRESS™

PLEASE RECYCLE
THIS PRODUCT IS RECYCLABLE

ISBN-13: 978-0-373-86174-3

Recycling programs
for this product may
not exist in your area.

MAKE IT LAST FOREVER

www.kimanipress.com

Printed in U.S.A.

Dear Reader,

Have you ever felt a sense of déjà vu? Has your soul ever reached out to someone like it knew the person? Have you ever met someone for the first time and knew immediately that person was meant to be in your life forever?

Community activist Karen Williams and rapper and movie star Darius "D-Roc" Rollins experience these feelings when a tragedy brings them together. Their souls seem to speak to one another and call out to one another even as everything in their everyday lives tells them they have absolutely nothing in common.

At its core, this novel flips the script on the old adage that people come into your life for a reason, a season or a lifetime. It gives that idea an extended-play hip-hop remix by asking what happens when the same person comes into your life across *several* lifetimes. Can we really make love last forever?

I hope you enjoy Darius and Karen's story. Be sure to let me know what you think of it! And be sure to pick up my November 2010 release, *Rivals in Paradise*.

Much love and peace,

Gwyneth

Acknowledgments

Trying to carve out a career in romance while also doing everything I need to do in my other career is a juggling act, to say the least. With national conferences to plan, papers to grade, graduate students to advise and deadlines ever looming, sometimes it seems like I will never get everything done! And oftentimes personal relationships get put on the back burner for my work and writing obligations. So I want to thank my family and friends for understanding when duty calls and I have to spend every waking moment in front of the laptop because the book is due. I especially want to thank my husband, Cedric Bolton, my mom, Donna Pough, my sisters Jennifer, Cassandra, Michelle and Tashina, my nieces Ashlee and Zaria and my nephew Michael. And to all the readers, thank you so much for all your e-mails and notes. When I'm writing and thinking about all the other things I want to be doing, it really helps to hear from you and be reminded that people are waiting to read the words I write. Knowing that you enjoy my novels and want to read more from me makes it all worthwhile. Finally, I want to thank the ladies of Live, Love, Laugh and Books for being the coolest Yahoo reading group on the planet! You ladies rock!

Chapter 1

"Woowee... I haven't seen this in ages. You couldn't tell me I wasn't sharp when I put this on. Girl, you should have seen me back in the day wearing this dress!" Amina Sunyetta held up an African-print micromini dress in front of herself and did a little wiggle.

Karen Williams looked up from the dusty corner of the attic. She had been doing her best not to sneeze as she helped her friend decide what items to take with her when she moved and which items to give to Goodwill. The attic in the Prospect Heights brownstone was cramped and cluttered with so many boxes that she doubted they would be done by nightfall. And with only two people there doing the work, being done by the end of the weekend seemed like wishful thinking, as well.

Amina held up a dress that almost looked like something the super-skinny 1960s supermodel Twiggy might have worn, *if* Twiggy had been a black nationalist, that is.

Amina's petite frame had clearly picked up a little weight over the years, but it wasn't too hard to imagine the short, dark-chocolate woman sporting the unique minidress in the past. In fact, from what Karen knew of Amina's exciting life, Karen would have been hard-pressed to pick anything she couldn't imagine Amina doing. The term *wild child* came easily to mind. She envisioned the woman, who now wore a pair of cherry-red sweatpants and a long black T-shirt with red rhinestones, sporting the little minidress.

Karen moved two of her long locs, which kept escaping from the scrunchie meant to hold back her multicolored locs and hopefully keep them from getting too dusty. She didn't have time to help her friend all weekend *and* also wash and retwist her hair. There were only so many hours in the day. And it was really important to her to help Amina. So the soothing ritual of washing, oiling and palm rolling would have to wait until next weekend.

Most of her locs—she refused to call them dreadlocks, because there was nothing dreadful about her hair in its natural state—were a deep, rich auburn color. But, mixed in here and there, she had splashes of other brighter, vibrant colors of copper, bronze and even one lone blond loc. Looking at her hair was like looking at fire, an element she felt strangely drawn to, at least figuratively. She didn't have a desire to be too close to real flames. But she felt like fire was the core of what a person needed to have in order to be able to enact change in the world.

Karen laughed as she stood, stretched and dusted her backside off. She gave Amina a smirk. "You actually fit into that little thing?"

Amina cut her eyes playfully. "I told you I was a stone-cold fox back in the day. Neat, petite and oh-so-sweet! I had all the conscious-'bout-it brothers after me trying to get me to make warriors with them for the revolution."

"All right now! What did sista Sonia tell us? '*Fucking* is *not* a revolutionary act,'" Karen playfully recited her favorite phrase from one of her favorite poems, Sonia Sanchez's "Queen of the Universe."

She had a deep fondness for sista poets from the 1970s, even though most of that stuff had been published before she was even born. She found the anthology *Black Fire* back when she was in high school and had searched out more women poets like Sonia Sanchez and Nikki Giovanni, devouring every line they ever wrote and moving on to Mari Evans, Carolyn M. Rodgers, June Jordan, Audre Lorde and countless others. A lot of times she felt like she was born a generation or two too late. At thirty years old, she often felt strangely connected to times that were before she was even born.

Amina guffawed. "And Sonia Sanchez ain't neva lied!" Amina put the dress down and stared at another box for a long time before she finally moved it over to Karen.

Karen glanced at it and knew that it must have been a box of Shemar's things. It had been six years since Amina's son and Karen's best friend, rapper Shemar Sunyetta, had been gunned down and murdered at the prime of his career. And it was still hard for either of them to deal with. That was part of the reason why Karen was there helping Amina clean out the attic. Amina still couldn't bring herself to deal with the loss of her only child, and going through his things was difficult.

"Thanks for spending part of your weekend helping me, Karen. I appreciate it. I really needed to get rid of some of this stuff before I move to South Carolina. I think I'm becoming a pack rat in my old age."

"With all this accumulation, I'm gonna go out on limb here and say you were a pack rat in your younger days, as well." Karen laughed. "Since I can't talk you out of moving to Myrtle Beach, I guess I can help you pack." She tried to keep an upbeat and playful tone.

Amina had always been like a second mother to her growing up, and she knew she would miss her. Since her only family had moved back down South to be closer to her mother's aging parents in Savannah, Georgia, she didn't have much family left in Brooklyn. She had lots of friends and a few stray cousins, but when it came to people who knew her in that way that only real family could, Amina was it. So Karen didn't want Amina to move. But she knew that Amina needed to finally get away from the house and the place that would always remind her of her dead son.

"Think of it this way. You'll have another fun place to visit. A place on the beach," Amina offered teasingly as she closed the box she'd been going through and pushed it near the other stacks of boxes she planned on donating to Goodwill.

"I just might take you up on that." Karen picked up another dusty box and started going through it. It looked like more of Amina's 1970s gear. There was a black leather jacket and a black beret along with some more funky minidresses and nice black patent-leather platform boots. The clothing appeared to be a few sizes larger than the tiny minidress Amina had been holding up. "I think I found some more of your clothes from back in the day. But they look a lot bigger than that little thing you were holding up before."

Karen picked up the red minidress with black-and-green zigzag stripes going up and down and around the material. Even though contemporary minidresses weren't her usual style at all, this retro minidress spoke to her. She could even visualize herself in it. And she had to admit she looked darn good in her head.

"This is cute. And it looks about my size. I could totally rock this! The retro look is back, you know." The dress had that classic 1970s look with the tapered waist and quarter sleeves that were flared at the end. She loved it.

Amina looked up, and a somewhat sad smile crossed her face. "That was my sister's. That must be a box of her things."

Karen picked up the jacket and tried it on along with the beret. "She must have been about my size. Was she a revolutionary back in the day also? What are you going to do with her stuff?"

Amina walked over. "Yes, my big sister was the one who brought me into the Black Liberation Army. I miss Karla something fierce! She passed away many years ago, but sometimes it feels like yesterday."

"Karla? You mean she didn't change her name like you did, *Becky?*" Sensing the sadness creeping into

Amina's voice, Karen teased her friend and playfully ducked the swing of Amina's arm that she knew was coming.

"My name is *Amina*. Didn't nobody get off the boat from the motherland named Becky or *Karen* for that matter. And no, Karla never changed her name. She kept it in honor of our father. His name was Karl, and she had been named for him."

Karen noticed the sadness that was starting to overcome Amina and tried to lighten the mood. "I think this minidress would look nice on me." She held the dress up in front of herself and gave a little shake. She was right. The dress seemed like it was made for her. She had never had one of those experiences her girlfriends talked about where an article of clothing or a fierce pair of shoes supposedly "spoke" to them from a catalog or store window and said "take me home" or "buy me." But that was the only way she could describe how she felt about the retro minidress. She wanted it. It was hers.

Karen smoothed the material of the dress and smiled. "As a matter of fact, this leather jacket looks nice on me, too, now that I think about it."

Amina started looking through the box. "You're welcome to anything you want in here. I still can't fit in Karla's clothing. She was always taller and thicker. As a matter of fact, she was about your size. But I have never seen you in a minidress. As a matter of fact, you rarely wear anything short. You wear those long crunchy granola crinkle skirts all the time or jeans and them damn Birkenstocks and those political T-shirts. I swear you must have a T-shirt for every political cause known to man." Amina rolled her eyes dramatically.

Karen looked down at the black T-shirt she was wearing that had her favorite Rebecca West quote from 1913 on it in purple letters. The T-shirt read "I have never been able to find out precisely what feminism is: I only know that people call me a feminist whenever I express sentiments that differentiate me from a doormat." She smiled because she was also wearing her favorite purple Converse sneakers, *not* Birkenstocks.

Karen held up her leg and wiggled her foot.

"Oh, yeah, I forgot to add your collection of colorful Converse sneakers to your wardrobe selections. Oops." Amina laughed. "This should be good though… Make sure you take a picture of yourself if you ever wear that minidress out someplace. This is something I have to see!" Amina started laughing.

"How you gonna call my clothes crunchy granola, and I'm helping you clean out your attic?" Karen sucked her teeth in feigned outrage as she put the minidress, leather jacket and black beret in her keeper pile along with an old sterling-silver name ring of Shemar's from back when they were in high school and neither one of them could afford the nice flashy gold ones with diamonds in them. She remembered when she and Shemar purchased the name rings the summer before her freshman year.

She kept digging through the box to see if any of the other clothes caught her eye and pulled out a book wrapped in kente cloth. The cloth was nice and thick and had an authentic feel to it. It felt old, not like the mass-produced stuff she purchased from the Harlem Market when she was feeling particularly ethnic. She unwrapped the cloth and found an old, worn, leather-bound book inside. It seemed to be older than the cloth. She flipped through it and noticed various handwritings throughout. It appeared to be a diary of some sort but one that different people had used.

She ran her hands across the leather. It had that soft, smooth, buttery feel that only really used leather could attain. She wanted to just put it in her keeper pile and not say anything. But something as personal as a diary or journal was probably not something Amina was going to want to get rid of. And it was really too bad because something inside of her was telling her to take the journal, to just put it in her keeper pile and take it home.

"Man, I haven't seen that thing in years! I remember when my sister, Karla, found that thing at a rummage sale. It was right before she met the man she called the love of her life, her soul mate." Amina gave a sarcastic chuckle. "As if such a thing even exists. And if they do exist, I'm doubly pissed off because I haven't found mine yet."

Karen laughed at Amina's suddenly disgusted expression. "So this journal belonged to Karla?"

"Yeah, she found it at a rummage sale at one of the churches where we held our free breakfast programs. I can't remember which one, though. I just know she started writing in it all the time after she met Daniel." Amina smiled and smacked her lips. "Now that was one fine man! He was one of those hustlers with a heart. Used to give money to the Black Liberation Army, give away turkeys in the hood to needy families during the holidays, toys to kids at Christmas, that kind of thing…

Real *smooth* brother… Used to say he couldn't get all the way down with the revolution because those berets would cramp his style."

Karen smiled and tilted her head to the side. "Um, seems like you had a little crush on your sister's man."

"Girl, every woman with blood pumping through her body had the hots for that man. But once he met Karla, he only had eyes for her. I'll tell you what, if soul mates do exist, those two were certainly soul mates. Once they got past their differences, they were inseparable. Heck, they were damn near magical. Made me sick!" Amina started laughing again.

"Sounds romantic. I'd sure like to find me a superfine, supersmooth brother to be my soul mate." Karen realized that her voice was getting wistful, and she actually meant the words she was saying.

Where the hell did that come from?

She frowned and rubbed her hand across the soft scuffed leather again. The last thing she needed was a soul mate. A soul mate would mean a relationship. And a relationship would mean time away from her beloved youth center. And all her time and energy was wrapped up in her "hood work," making the neighborhood a safer and more productive place for the youth. She didn't have time for love or a relationship. And she certainly didn't have time for any kind of soul mate.

Perish the thought!

So why did she all of a sudden want one more than she wanted the money to buy all new computers for the technology room in the Shemar Sunyetta Youth Center?

She scrunched up her face as she continued to rub

the journal and let the leather lull her into thoughts of finding *the one*. "What are you going to do with her journal?"

"I don't know. It doesn't seem right to just give it to Goodwill. Karla found her man after she found the journal. I had that thing for years after she and Daniel were killed in that freak automobile accident back in 1980." Amina shuddered and closed her eyes for a moment. She frowned as she stared at the journal before shrugging and continuing.

"The journal didn't bring me a soul mate or even a halfway decent man to warm my bed at night." Amina rested her finger on her chin in contemplation. "In fact, since she died and I took her book, all I got was eight years of Reagan, four years of Bush, the end of the Black Liberation Army, the blissful, almost willful ignorance of the Clinton years, a revolutionary's worst nightmare in eight years of W and the murder of my only child. That journal has probably been jinxing me! Nothing has gone my way personally or politically since I took it. I don't know where that journal is going, but it's not going with me to South Carolina and messing up my new start. Call me superstitious if you want!"

"Hey, but we have change we can believe in now. So maybe the tide is turning, at least politically." Karen shook her head and laughed. Then she realized that if Amina didn't want the journal, maybe she'd be willing to let her take it.

"I could take the journal off your hands. I want to read all about your sister's love affair with her soul mate." She flipped through the pages, noting the different handwritings and the hearts drawn on some of the pages throughout. "It looks like a lot of different owners have written in it. Maybe I can live vicariously through them, because Lord knows I don't have time to have a love life."

"You can have the journal. Maybe it'll bring you a man." Amina twisted up her face and stuck out her tongue. "Because Lord knows you need one." Amina laughed and ducked when Karen threw the kente cloth at her.

"Girl, you better go on and get you some love! Don't wake up my age and alone. It's not a fun place to be. Whatever happened to that Saul guy you met in college that used to work with you at the center? Didn't you and he have something going on? What happened with him?" Amina frowned. "I never really liked him, but he seemed like he was stuck to you like glue."

"Saul finally saved up enough money to take a trip to the motherland. You know he was Mr. Africa *via* Alabama." Karen laughed. "But we weren't a good match. He needs his African Queen, and I hope he finds her over there. I just miss the fact that I could really count on him to help out at the center. And the sex wasn't bad when I had an itch that needed scratching. He was all right as an FWB."

"What the hell is an FWB?"

"A friend with benefits!" Karen chuckled.

Amina paused, and her eyes widened when Karen told her what it meant. "Girl, he was just taking up space and keeping you from finding the man you were supposed to be with. But I might have to look into this FWB thing a little more." Amina laughed. "You wait and see. I'm gonna call you from my house on the beach and tell you all about the fine young hottie that's gonna fall in love with me and knock me off my feet. I'm gonna get me a young tender roni."

"Watch out now, cougar! I see I'm gonna have to keep you away from the youth center. You might start scoping out the youth to give them more than just a little hope and inspiration."

Amina laughed. "I like them young, but not *that* young! They have to be at least drinking age. And since I'm a black woman, that would be *panther,* not *cougar.* Get it right, girlfriend!"

Both women cracked up then.

"You're a hot mess, Amina. A hot mess!"

"And don't you forget it. Come on, girl. I need some lunch if I'm gonna tackle the rest of this. Let's go downstairs and eat. I know you'll be talking about how I worked you to death and didn't feed you."

Karen got up and followed Amina down the stairs. But their conversation about love struck a chord. She had just turned thirty. Was it time for her to find a man? She shook off the thought.

"You know me so well. I sure will talk about how you worked me like a slave and didn't offer me a sip of water. Not to mention it's hotter than hell up in here. You would pick the start of summer to want to clean out your attic and move down South. Only you, Amina, only you!"

"Girl, stop complaining and come on!"

They laughed and continued walking. Karen barely realized that she still had the journal in her hands.

Darius "D-Roc" Rollins stood in the finished basement of the home he'd purchased for his grandmother, not really listening to the chatter that was going on around him. He still couldn't believe that his younger cousin—his only cousin, who had been just like a little brother to him—was dead.

He had dispensed with his normal entourage for the funeral and was thinking about taking a break from his boys for a little longer. He just needed a change. He needed a break from everything that had kept him away from his family for years.

And the way he was feeling about the loss of his cousin, he really didn't want a large group of people just hanging around him following his every move. The group mentality had lost its appeal. Most of his core entourage were his homeboys anyway, so they took the respite as a chance to visit with their own families.

He looked around the room. The newly finished room had state-of-the-art electronics, a minitheater, wall-to-wall cream carpet, plush rust-colored sofas and light olive-green paint on the walls. The large mahogany sofa tables, end tables and table and chairs off in the corner tied the entire room together. It was actually his first time seeing the room since it had been remodeled. He was glad that he had surprised his grandmother by paying for it and hiring someone to make sure no detail was left to chance. The large space was now a family recreation room that was perfect for entertaining large groups. He'd had it remodeled a year ago for his grandmother's birthday, thinking it would keep his cousin home more. He had no idea then that they would be standing in the same room mourning the loss of the boy.

How could you account for an eighteen-year-old

college student with his entire life in front of him being gunned down in a neighborhood that he no longer lived in but couldn't seem to stay away from? How did a person come to grips with the fact that no matter how much money he sent home to get his family out of the hood and keep his cousin out of the streets, the streets still managed to claim his cousin?

He looked around at all the faces standing around the basement, eating the food he'd had catered for the repast. The sad thing was that most of the people there probably couldn't care less about Frankie. Most of them were only there to get a glimpse of "D-Roc." Some had even asked for autographs and some had snapped pictures with their cell phones.

Pathetic. He didn't regret his celebrity by any means. But he did regret the way people behaved because of it.

"It's good to have you home, son." His grandmother came and stood by him.

The tall, bronze-complexioned woman with her salt-and-pepper hair curled softly around her face looked older than she ever had. Her eyes were puffy and bloodshot, and he could tell she'd been crying again. It broke his heart to see her so torn apart. She'd raised him after his mother was murdered, and when her youngest daughter had gotten pregnant as a teenager, she'd essentially taken on raising that child, too—Frankie. Burying Frankie probably felt as bad to her as when she'd buried Darius's mother.

"I'm sorry I didn't come home more often. Maybe if I had—"

"Don't you go blaming yourself, Darius! Wasn't

nothing you could do to keep Frankie out of them streets. Lord knows we tried. He just wouldn't listen. He wouldn't have listened to you either."

"How you know that, Mama? He might have. He looked up to Darius." His aunt Janice was only six years older than him. She'd had Frankie when she was eighteen. She was also tall with a bronze complexion and looked like a younger version of his grandmother. She wore an expensive weave with jet-black hair hanging well down her back. Despite her tears and sorrow at the moment, she was still in her typical perpetually angry state of being.

Unfortunately, this time she had a right to be angry with him.

Darius knew he should have done more to make sure his cousin stayed away from dangerous situations. It took more than buying a nice big house in New Hyde Park and moving the family to the safer Nassau County suburb. It took more than footing the bill for private school and guaranteeing a full ride to college.

Neither he nor Frankie had ever had a father figure— just Grandma and Janice. What Frankie needed—hell, what the little thug who had shot and killed Frankie probably needed, for that matter—was someone there who understood what it meant to be a young man in the hood, someone willing to be there and talk to him and talk him out of foolishness.

All the money in the world didn't make up for time. It was funny how it took tragedy to bring some lessons home. For the first time in his life, he knew more than ever that nothing beat time. The death of his cousin brought that lesson home with enough poignancy to last several lifetimes.

His chest felt heavy. So much pressure was building up; it felt as if it was going to cave in and all of his insides would be exposed. Something had to give, and he had to let it out or he knew he might just explode.

He tightened up, holding it in. He couldn't break down. He had to be a rock for his grandmother and aunt. He let out a stuttered breath and then another.

Frankie was dead.

It was his fault, even if he hadn't held the gun. He needed to own up to that and not cry over it like a little boy.

Man up!

That's what he needed to do. At thirty years old, he was the man of his family. He needed to start doing more than throw his money around to prove it. He loosened his tie. The central air was blasting, but he still felt closed in wearing the suit and tie he'd worn to the funeral.

"You're right, Janice. I should have been here for Frankie. He needed me, and I failed him."

"I'm glad you know it! Too bad it's too late." Janice glared at him before cutting her eyes.

"Janice, stop that! This child is grieving just like we are. It's not fair for us to put this all on him. It's not fair, and it's not right. He did all he could for Frankie. We all did." Grandma's voice cracked, and she started sobbing again.

Darius wrapped his arms around her and held her as she cried. He held her together and tried to keep everything he felt inside from tumbling out.

He could just see someone with a fancy cell phone or digital camera shooting a video of him breaking down. And he could just see the video showing up on YouTube if he gave in to what he was feeling and cried—if he let the pain take over.

The tenuous street cred he had as a so-called positive rapper-turned-Hollywood-movie-star would be gone if someone caught him slipping and he ended up bawling like a little baby on the Internet.

He shook his head and frowned.

Street cred.

That's the reason Frankie was dead. He hadn't wanted to leave the hood behind. He'd wanted to show that he was still down. There had to be a way to be down and not end up in the ground. Hell, he didn't want to forget where he came from any more than his cousin had. He'd given back financially to lots of good causes and charities in the hood.

He threw money at the hood, the same way he'd thrown money at his cousin.

"Can't talk now, Frankie, I'm on set about to shoot a scene. I'll call you later. Hope you like the new wheels."

"Gotta hit the studio, man. Tell your moms and Grandma I said hi. I'll try and call y'all this weekend."

He wasn't even going to think about all the times he'd let calls from his cousin go straight to voice mail because he was busy with a sexy model or Hollywood starlet. He had dropped the ball, and his cousin had paid the price.

"I'm going to stick around for a little while. I'm

between films, and I can put off the studio for a min—"

"Oh, don't stick around now! We don't need you now! Go back to Hollywood. Go back to your busy life!" Janice choked out in an angry hiss. "Frankie needed you. You couldn't make time for him...." Her voice trailed off and she bit back angry tears.

He wasn't mad at his aunt. She needed someone to blame. Hell, even he blamed himself. So why should he expect any different from her?

"I'm thinking about devoting some time down in the old neighborhood, some time in East New York. There are a couple of youth centers. I could spend some time... I could try and honor Frankie's memory."

He had to do something.

"Oh, son, you don't need to be down there. It's dangerous. Anything could happen. You should just go on back to your life where it's safe." The worried expression on his grandmother's face tugged at his heart.

He knew the last thing she needed to worry about was the possibility of burying yet another child.

"You don't have to worry about me, Grandma. I'll be fine." He wanted to say that he wouldn't be involved with the kinds of things that his cousin had been involved in. But he knew that would have set his aunt off unnecessarily.

At the end of the day, it didn't matter what Frankie had been involved in. Darius had failed him.

"The old neighborhood? Why would you want to be down there? No one wants you down there. Go back to Hollywood, Darius! I can't believe you're going to use my child's death as a part of some bullshit publicity stunt!" The ugliness of his aunt's voice and the distrusting glare in her eyes shook him to his core.

When had it gotten this bad? When did his own family actually forget who he really was? The fact that his aunt could even accuse him of such a thing let him know that he had really dropped the ball where they were concerned.

"That's not what I'm doing, Jan… You should know that. In spite of everything… You should know…" He shook his head. The basement was starting to close in on him and that sinking about-to-cave-in feeling in his chest had him thinking if he didn't get out of there soon he really would end up broken down and sobbing on the floor. He took a deep breath. He needed air, so he walked away from them.

"Son, don't go. Don't let Janice upset you like this. We know you, son. We know you! We love you." His grandmother's voice trailed off as he walked up the stairs.

Even though he knew he could never make things right for his cousin, the tragic loss demanded that he try, demanded that he do something.

Chapter 2

Two weeks after helping Amina clean out the attic, the woman Karen thought of as her "other mother" moved to Myrtle Beach. Karen had gone out to dinner with Amina the other night and said her tearful goodbye. Even though it felt like her connection to her deceased best friend was gone, she still had the youth center to hold on to.

It was Monday, and Karen walked up to the Shemar Sunyetta Youth Center with the same sense of optimism she started each week with. Her building was two stories of prime Brooklyn real estate—two stories of space, opportunity and possibility.

No matter how things had gone the week before, she started each day of the week with a continued steadfast belief in the change she could evoke in people's lives. Her mother had always called it her stubborn streak. But Karen thought of it as sheer determination.

She was determined to make a difference all day, every day.

As Karen lifted the gate at the entrance to the youth center, Dicey "Divine" Stamps walked up and lifted the gate to her storefront palm-reading spot, Divine Intuition. It was right next door to Karen's youth center. Ever since the quirky woman opened up the store a year ago, she had been trying to get Karen to come in for a reading.

Karen always said no. While she might have embraced a sort of eclectic style when it came to hair and clothing, she was *really* traditional when it came to certain things. She didn't do the woo-woo stuff! Period.

"My offer to read you still stands. I'll give you half off my normal rates." Dicey hefted up her gate with a smile. The tall, almost Amazon-like woman had deep, dark skin and wore her long curly hair in thick goddess braids. The braids were wrapped around her head and had an almost crownlike appearance. She always wore African-print goddess gowns. Today she had on a short-sleeved long dress made of mud cloth.

"Girl, you know I don't believe in all of that." For some reason, she thought about the journal that she had taken from Amina's house and how she had felt so compelled to take it with her. She hadn't picked up the journal since she took it, so she had no idea why it popped into her head at that moment.

"Don't you want to know?" Dicey said in a way that almost made Karen think she knew what was going on in Karen's head.

Confusion crossed her face as she looked at Dicey.

Dicey chuckled as if she were amused with herself.

"Don't you want to know what's in your future, dear one?"

Karen laughed. "I already know what's in my future, lots of irritated teens if I don't get in here and get things ready. The summer is a busy time of year for a youth center."

"I'm seeing love in your near future. Don't you want to come and find out when you're going to meet your soul mate?"

Karen stopped laughing then and stared at Dicey really hard. She thought about the journal again and the story Amina had told her about Karla and Daniel. She shook her head, both to clear it and to say no.

"All right then, but my offer stands whenever you stop being afraid and you're ready to embrace your destiny, dear one." Dicey offered a melodious laugh before heading into her shop.

Karen unlocked the door to the center and went about her day.

"If you can't follow the rules then you won't be able to come here again." A familiar sadness began to creep into Karen's heart as she kept her stern frown focused on Clarence.

She had pulled him into her back office after she caught him trying to sell a marijuana blunt to one of the other young men. She went back and forth in her mind about the right thing to do and decided against calling the police. She hoped she wouldn't regret that decision.

The boy was only fifteen, and already she sensed it might be too late for him. But she didn't think being sent back to juvenile detention would have helped him either. She knew that she might have been able to reach him eventually. But if he was bringing drugs into her center, then there was really nothing she could do. She couldn't condone that.

No way.

She leaned back a little in her rolling office chair. The high-end office chair was one of the items in her office that she had spent a little extra money on. The rest of the furnishings were low-end Office Max cherry-stained plywood. But at least everything matched and looked professional. Her office was the only space in the center that she had cut back on when it came to furniture. She really invested all of her money and her time in making the center a nice, welcoming space for the youth, a space where they could come and get away from the lures of the street.

Allowing Clarence to remain at the center would jeopardize everything she was trying to accomplish. And more than just Clarence's future was at stake. So many young people needed the space that the center offered. Still, anytime she had to sacrifice one for the whole it hurt. She really wanted to save them all.

"That's cool. Whatever, yo, whatever." Clarence shrugged his shoulders and twisted his face in a harsh manner.

The bravado he put up didn't fool Karen at all. She knew that he cared more than he let on. And if she could give him another chance she would have. But he had a long way to go before he stopped letting the wrong folks influence him.

"I'll tell your parole officer that it just didn't work

out here. But I'm sure he'll be able to find another place for you."

"That's jacked up, Ms. Williams. You pretend like you care and that you want to give us a chance. But then you just throw us out 'cause we mess up. I said I didn't mean to—"

"You didn't mean to get caught. That's all." Karen ran her hands through her locs.

Was she being too hard on Clarence? Could she allow him to stick around? She thought about the other young people at the center—the ones Clarence had tried to sell drugs to.

No. No, he had to go.

"Whatever, Ms. Williams. You just like everybody else. You ain't really trying to give a brother a chance. You just talkin', you don't mean that shit you be saying."

"That's not true, Clarence! You have to take some responsibility here. That's the problem. You're not taking responsibility. You just want to blame others."

Clarence pushed his chair back harshly and leaped out of his seat, knocking the cherry-stained wooden chair he'd been sitting on to the ground. "This place was wack anyway. I got better stuff to do with my time than waste it here."

"Clarence, don't leave mad. Let's talk about the other options available to you. I can't let you continue to hang out here. But there are—"

"Man, fuck this! I'm out." Clarence went bursting out the door.

Torn between following him and hoping that his leaving would help things remain on an even keel, Karen took a deep breath and placed her head on her desk instead. She wondered if she had done him any favors by just barring him from the center and not calling the cops. She told herself it was just weed. But she wondered if calling the cops on him would have ensured that he didn't move on to other drugs in the future.

As she mentally went over the reasons yet again why Clarence had to go, the phone on her desk rang, jolting her.

She picked up the phone and paused before answering.

"Shemar Sunyetta Youth Center, Karen Williams speaking." Dragging a halfway pleasant greeting out was easier than making her voice sound like she meant it, so she settled for brevity.

"Hello, Ms. Williams. My name is Cullen Stamps, and I represent Darius Rollins. He's a rapper. You might have heard of him?"

"Yes, I've heard of *D-Roc*." Twirling her locs with a pencil, she waited for some sort of explanation.

Who in the world hadn't heard of hip-hop's golden boy turned Hollywood movie star? A person would have to live under a rock not to have heard of D-Roc, especially a person in the East New York section of Brooklyn. He was the boy from the hood who had made it out and done good.

"Yes, well. He is interested in devoting some time to your center as a way of giving back. You might have heard that his young cousin was just murdered and—"

Cutting people off was rude, but she didn't have the patience to let him go on.

"Don't tell me… He wants to spend a few hours here

as a part of some publicity stunt, right? My goodness, what celebrities won't do for a little bit of attention. Is he really trying to turn his cousin's death into some kind of image or marketing opportunity? Sheesh." She clicked her tongue in disgust.

Not that her center couldn't use a little free publicity, but she was really protective of the kids, and allowing a celebrity—no matter how fine that celebrity was—to use them wasn't going to happen on her watch.

"Ms. Williams, I know that you are probably overworked, and we certainly appreciate the good work you're doing with the youth. That's why Mr. Rollins is determined to volunteer at your center. He has researched several, and he likes what you've done in such a short period of time with so few resources. He intends to volunteer a large amount of time while he is between films. He's even holding off getting right back in the studio for his much-anticipated third album. Against my better judgment, I might add. To be frank, Ms. Williams, you really could stand to gain a lot from his presence at your little center. The publicity would work both ways. He'd put you on the radar, and you might just get more donations for your little cause."

Each time the man said the word *little* in reference to her center—her life's work—her skin crawled. If this was the type of person D-Roc had representing him then she didn't want any part of him.

"Tell Mr. Rollins thanks, but no, thanks. My *little* center can get along just fine."

Something about the manager's slimy voice made her skin crawl. She didn't like Cullen Stamps. And no amount of free publicity was worth dealing with the smarmy man. D-Roc clearly surrounded himself with questionable people. And that was all the more reason not to be lulled by a shot at some free publicity.

"Well, now. Ms. Williams—"

"Well, now, what? I'm not interested in helping Mr. Rollins enhance his so-called positive image by letting him waltz through my center and these kids' lives for his own grandstanding. Goodbye!"

It felt so good to hang up the phone in his face. But as soon as she did it she realized that she might have done so in haste. Free publicity might mean more donations. She really could have used the publicity, because in these economic times the grants weren't coming in as frequently as they used to.

D-Roc personified the words *media darling*. Not since Will Smith had a rapper been able to totally enrapture the American public. He certainly was loved, and he might have brought some of that love to her center. But if he hired slime like Stamps, it probably wasn't worth it. She was right to turn Stamps down.

She was trying to instill values in the youth, not slick Hollywood images and media-induced frenzies. And there was something about the snarky sound of Stamps's voice that rubbed her the wrong way. After the run-in with Clarence, she just wanted to be able to tear into someone. Stamps just picked the wrong time to call and plead D-Roc's case.

The rest of the day went on pretty much uneventfully, and Karen couldn't help but feel glad. Usually running a center and doing "hood work," as she liked to call her activism in the community, made for more drama-filled days than she desired. But most days, when she could look at the kids and know that she was keeping them off the streets and exposing them to things and ideas that would help them stay off the street, she knew that it was all worth it.

After her very small group of staff and volunteers left and she got the last kid away from a computer and out the door, Karen went over to lock the door so that no one else could come in while she worked on some more grant applications for a little while. Before she could lock the door, it came bursting open, pushing her back. She looked up to tell whoever it was that the center was closed for the day.

Depending on who had so rudely barged in, her tone might have been pleasant or it might have been filled with attitude; she reserved the verdict until she got a good glimpse.

Looking at the muscled form and devil-may-care smirk that crossed a deliciously chocolate-brown face, she realized that she suddenly couldn't decide. Standing in front of her, in a pair of jeans, polo shirt, expensive sneakers and a fitted New York Yankees cap, was the most gorgeous man she had ever seen.

Stunned, she could not find her words.

D-Roc apparently wasn't one to give up easily.

Darius Rollins came into the youth center all set to pull every trick in his playbook in order to make this Karen Williams person allow him to volunteer at her youth center. The thought of just finding another youth center in which to volunteer never even crossed his mind. He'd researched the few youth centers around his old neighborhood, and he liked this one. Even though

he hadn't known Shemar Sunyetta personally, he felt that
the fact the center was named for the murdered rapper
was a sign of some sort.

He honestly didn't know why he bothered paying
Cullen. The man couldn't get him a volunteer gig! He
could only surmise that if it wasn't something Cullen
could make a commission off of, then he wasn't pressed
to work as hard.

Cullen had said that the woman running the center
was a bitch, and she wasn't trying to be helpful at all.
Darius just figured Cullen lacked finesse. Darius knew
he had to go down to the center and work his magic
on the woman. Cullen had said that the woman was
probably some uptight, ugly prude with an attitude who
hated men. Darius didn't care what she was or how she
looked. He'd have her eating out of his hands in no time,
and he'd be able to finally do something to honor his
cousin's memory.

Looking at the brown-skinned beauty with stunning
crinkled auburn and copper locs, he had to say Cullen
had gotten it all wrong. Yet again! The woman who
glanced up at him with large chocolate-brown eyes,
flawless toasted-cinnamon skin and lush red lips
was—in a word—beautiful. She was of medium height
and had a figure that was stacked in all the right places.
She wore a pair of jeans with holes in them, and he
got the sense that hers weren't purchased that way. She
also wore a black-and-white "No More Prisons" T-shirt
and white Converse sneakers. The jeans fit her curves
perfectly, and the T-shirt told him a little something
about her possible politics.

She intrigued him immensely. At least he wouldn't

have to fake it when he flirted with her. Because—seeing her—he knew exactly which tactic he was going for. Strong-arm tactics were out. Smooth-talking-mack-dropping-game-slinging skills were in and definitely more in line with how he planned to play it.

"Hello" was the extent of what he could manage to utter as he took in her overwhelming beauty. His heart actually felt as if it had stalled and kick-started as he really looked at her this time. Shaking his head in an effort to clear the foggy uneasiness that had started to creep into his being, Darius cleared his throat.

She had glanced up at him when he walked into the center, and she was still looking at him. Her big, brown eyes slightly widened, and she finally blinked several times in rapid succession.

He guessed by her wide-eyed, prolonged stare that she might have been experiencing a reaction very similar to his own. But what would be the best way to find out if she was?

"So, you're Karen Williams." He let her name roll off his tongue, and he could have sworn he tasted each syllable.

She blinked and shook her head. The dazed look in her eyes was quickly replaced by a stern expression. "Yes, I am. And we are just about to close, Mr. Rollins. I don't know why you're here. I've given my answer to your request to your very condescending manager."

So she knew who he was. That could be a good thing. Maybe she was a fan. However, if she were a fan, she probably wouldn't have declined his offer to volunteer. He glanced at her and found her lips twisted to the side and her left eye slightly slanted; the entire look was a mixture of incredulity and disgust. Okay, so maybe it wasn't such a good thing, and she definitely wasn't a fan. He could deal with that. He firmed his resolve to woo her.

"I apologize for whatever Cullen did or said to turn you off. But I would like to speak with you about me volunteering here. I read about the good work you're doing, and I really want to help out. In fact, seeing your pretty face is enough to make a brother long for community service." He gave her his very best Hollywood smile, his most sultry and seductive leading-man smile.

Judging by the extra dose of sour she added to her expression, he probably could have left that last sentence out. But it wasn't a lie. Seeing her made him want to volunteer there now more than ever.

"Yeah, whatever. Listen, it's late, and I've been here all day. I don't have time to talk with you now."

"How about I take you out for a bite to eat, and we can get to know one another. You know you can fill me in on how we can best make use of my very generous offer to volunteer here. And I can fill you in on all my many talents and the amount of publicity and donations I can bring to your center. You know, the perfect win-win situation."

The beautiful woman arched her left eyebrow and twisted her lips again. "I don't think so… I don't know." She gave him a hesitant once-over, and he let himself hope that she was reconsidering.

"Okay, you can come in tomorrow morning when we open. We can talk about it then. Good night, Mr. Rollins."

Although the last thing he wanted to do was leave there without making a better connection with the lovely Karen Williams, Darius realized that he probably wasn't going to get very far with her that evening. Good thing he was so determined to do everything in his power to make her say yes. He'd have plenty of time to get her to think better of him.

"Solid. That's cool. We've got plenty of time to get to know one another and to connect. Plenty of time."

She stared at him, and he thought he saw a glimmer of something in her eyes. He almost wanted to kick himself for giving up so quickly. He might have had more of a chance than he thought he did at wearing her down that evening. Dang.

Then, just as quickly as the sparkle flashed in her eyes, it was gone and replaced with "sista-tude."

"Yeah, well, whatever. I'll see you in the morning. Peace."

Giving the beautiful and sexy woman one last glance, he begrudgingly turned to leave. It hardly seemed like the right thing to do, and everything inside of him screamed, *"Stay until she at least warms up to you!"* He hoped that he'd get the opportunity.

One thing he was sure of was that he wouldn't give up until he accomplished what he wanted. The other thing was that he was no longer sure if exactly what he wanted was a chance to volunteer, a chance to get to know Karen or both.

Chapter 3

Karen leaned back and tried to calm the rapid—almost erratic—beating of her heart. It had been all she could manage just to string words together to speak to D-Roc. While she had never been one to be starstruck or anything like that, she figured that must have been the reason why her skin felt clammy and all the air seemed to be gone. She was damn near hyperventilating because she had seen a rap star.

No, that couldn't be it. She had been around rappers before. Her now-deceased best friend had been a rapper, and she'd hung out with him and other rappers lots of times. But she had never been around D-Roc. And now she wondered how in the heck she was going to manage being around him if he managed to sweet-talk her into letting him volunteer at the center.

The brother was fine. She had seen his shirtless, perfectly chiseled torso on countless magazine covers, and it always made her stop and gaze longingly. And the photos of the ripples and muscles in his chest and those bulging biceps of his always had a way of making her heart rate rise. But she had no idea that seeing the man in person—fully clothed—would almost send her into heart failure! Good Lord! The man gave new meaning to the phrase "sex appeal."

But it was more than that. Something deep inside of her was calling out to him. She felt it as sure as she ever felt anything in her life. And that scared her.

Locking up the center, she started off down the block to the bus stop. The evening walk usually gave her a fair amount of time to clear her head, especially in the summer. Yet this evening the only thing her mind wanted to focus on was D-Roc. On second thought, she wished it was only her mind stuck on the rapper and actor.

Seeing him did something weird to her. Her heart felt—funny. Her soul felt—light, almost airy. And the other physical reactions…the dampness that made her wish she'd worn a panty liner and the tight ache in her nipples. She wasn't even trying to analyze those. She was not some groupie chicken-head, but she swore it took everything inside of her not to run up on the brother and tongue him down.

Not cool.

"I know you not gonna walk home at this hour of the night?" The deep and sexy voice that came from behind her would have made her break off running on any other evening.

She turned and got caught up in the deep brown eyes of Darius Rollins. The lopsided grin that highlighted the dimple in his left cheek didn't help matters. She made an effort not to look down, because she knew it would only compound matters due to his toned and muscular physique.

"Can I give you a lift?"

"I don't get into cars with strangers."

"I'm not a stranger." He took another step closer, and all semblance of personal space was gone.

His eyes glimmered, and for a brief second he looked different. A person flashed in her mind—another man wearing a 1970s-style polyester suit with a funky print shirt and perfect Afro. The tall man with a lean and muscular build looked different. But she would have put money on the fact that the personality and the cocky smile were one in the same.

Shaking her head in an effort to try and clear her obvious delusion, Karen took a step back.

With his cocksure grin aimed dead at her, Darius took a step forward.

If she had her Mace out she would have considered spraying him with it. She would have considered it, but she never would have done it. The tingling in her gut and the sudden goose pimples popping up on her skin wouldn't have allowed her to really hurt the pesky man.

"Are you always so annoying?" Dang, her voice sounded husky and wanton even to her own ears. She wondered what it sounded like to him.

Judging by the self-assured glimmer in his eyes and the flash of arrogance in his smile, he had picked up on it all right. Leaning closer, he actually let his hand brush her face.

An electric charge coursed through her body, and a sudden case of dry mouth overwhelmed her.

Are my palms sweating? Sheesh, my freaking palms are sweating!

Swallowing a couple of times and failing at not making it look like she was taking gulps of air in the process, she slanted her eyes.

"I'm not trying to be annoying. I just want to give you a ride home. A pretty woman such as yourself shouldn't be walking out here alone."

"It's summertime, and there's still a little daylight left. Plus, I'm just walking to the bus stop. I do it all the time."

"Well, today I would love it if you'd do me the honor of letting me see you safely to your door. A pretty woman like you shouldn't have to ride public transportation. It's the least I can do."

She couldn't help but cut her eyes. How did he manage to make chauvinism sexy?

Oh, hell, no!

Chauvinism was *so* not sexy, no matter how much he drank her in with his dark brown bedroom eyes.

Uh-uh. No.

"If I have managed to make it to the bus stop and home by my little lonesome all these years without a big strong man to make sure I got there, then surely I can continue to do so," she said in an overly sweet voice before flipping back to her normal tone. "Your showing up at my youth center didn't alter the universe or anything. I'm still the same grown-ass woman I was when I woke up this morning."

Darius really let his eyes do the talking then. The

brown probes gave her an up-and-down appraisal that left her feeling fully and truly exposed. She felt like he could see inside of her, knowing her thoughts, wants and desires.

"You ain't neva lied about that! But check it, let me just see you home. I'll sleep so much better knowing that you're safe. Remember, I just had a cousin killed in this neighborhood. Just let me do this." He held out his hand, and in a moment of complete and utter craziness that she would have never anticipated in a million years, she took it and followed him to his car. As soon as her hand touched his, a jolt of overwhelming awareness went through her, and she knew that she was in big trouble.

As soon as Karen's hand touched his, a spark of something Darius couldn't name ran through him. Trying to ignore the loud, incessant beating of his heart, Darius gave a quick sideways glance to the sexy, vibrant, out-of-this-world dynamic beauty holding his hand. In a matter of a few minutes, he felt like he never wanted to let her go.

And he couldn't stop staring at her for anything. He actually stood in front of his car for at least a couple of seconds trying to figure out why for a split second she looked like a different woman. He could have sworn her auburn and copper locs morphed into a 1970s Angela Davis Afro for a minute.

Yeah, Karen Williams had him tripping for real. He needed to hurry up and get her home so he could figure out how one look at her made him want to spend all his time getting to know every single thing about her.

Once they were both settled into the car, he turned to her. "So where to, beautiful?"

"You're going to regret offering me a ride." She gave him a saucy grin. "I live all the way in South Brooklyn, in the Boerum Hill neighborhood. Betcha now you wish you had let me take the bus." A lyrical laugh escaped her lips.

He laughed and winked at her. "Actually, my place, when I'm in town, is in South Brooklyn, as well. I have a loft in Cobble Hill. That's about as close as this Brooklyn boy was going to get to Manhattan. If I'm in the city, I'm in my borough."

She gave a soft chuckle. "Didn't want to get a place in money-making Manhattan, huh?"

"Manhattan makes it—" he started.

"—but Brooklyn takes it!" They finished the old party chant together and laughed.

"So see, it's fate. I was meant to spend more time with you tonight." He started the car and realized that he actually believed what he just said. He wasn't running game or anything.

Once Darius had dropped Karen off at her apartment, he still couldn't get her out of his head. It was almost as if she was on a continuous loop set to repeat indefinitely. Her smile, her luminous eyes, her scent...

Damn, her scent was like honey, hibiscus, dew and a shot of warm desire. He could imagine living the rest of his life with nothing but her scent for nourishment. It almost felt as if something snapped to life in him as soon as he got close enough to get a good whiff. The close quarters in the car had been hell. He'd wanted to pull over and pull her into his arms.

The sharp ring of the phone jolted him out of his reverie. When he made the mad dash to catch it and found that it was his manager, Cullen Stamps, he wished that he had just let it ring.

"So now that that hard-edged bitch has turned you down, are you over your need to spend time at that little youth center and get back in the studio? You don't have a lot of time to record the album before your next film begins shooting. In this business, you have to strike while you're hot. You don't have time to waste at that youth center. Send them a donation in your cousin's name and call it a day."

No *hello* or *how're you doing* for Cullen. Just straight to business.

Hesitation and hiding never appealed to Darius, so he was up-front about his lack of success. But he also let Cullen know that he didn't intend to give up. In fact, he was more dedicated than ever to make this happen.

"I really like Karen, and I admire what she's doing with the youth. I might try and figure out a way to volunteer at her center whenever I have a break in my schedule. You know, set up something ongoing and permanent."

"What do you mean whenever you have a break in your schedule? There is no such thing as a break. You don't have a break now! You should be in the studio. Time is money!"

"I mean just what I said. Hey, it's for a good cause. It's for my cousin's memory. It's the least I can do, and I'm going to do it." He didn't even worry about the edge in his voice. Cullen needed to hear that edge and know to back the hell up.

"Do I have to remind you that every minute you spend at that center is time away from the studio? And what about the fact that you running around in the hood without folks to protect you isn't exactly the smartest idea. You may not be as successful as Will Smith yet, but you're still a highly recognizable person. You wouldn't want to end up just like your cousin by trying to do something in his memory."

Darius could literally feel his face twisting in anger. East New York was his hood. He'd be damned if he started walking around with bodyguards in his own neighborhood. That wasn't going to happen. And for Cullen to insinuate that he needed bodyguards or a damn entourage? That was the height of disrespect, and he wasn't having it.

"I can take care of myself." His tone moved from hard-edged to straight-up harsh. And sometimes with Cullen that was exactly what it took.

"If you say so—"

"I say so."

"Well, what about recording? We don't have a lot of—" Cullen's entire demeanor changed, but it still wasn't enough for Darius. He had to cut Cullen off and nip it all in the bud.

"It's all good, Cullen. Chill! I'll just cut back on the partying." It struck Darius how much he really meant that only after the words had fallen out of his mouth. The only important thing for him at that moment was honoring his cousin's memory and being able to spend more time with Karen.

"I guess if you can manage to stay on track with the recording then it should be fine."

"It'll be more than fine. Look man, I'm gonna catch some z's or try to, anyway. I'll holla later."

"But—"

Darius just hung up the phone on Cullen. He'd made up his mind to pursue the lovely Ms. Williams. If nothing else, he had to figure out why he hadn't been able to stop thinking about her since he met her. And why he felt as if he'd known her forever when he only met her a few hours ago. Yeah, once he figured all that out, he'd be cool.

Cullen hung up the phone and counted to ten in order to stop himself from throwing the damn thing across the room. He must have underestimated both of them. He just knew that his phone call to the girl had turned her off enough to make her not want to deal with Darius at all. Why did Darius have to go down there and see her?

He sighed. He needed a Plan B in place in case Darius didn't bend the way he wanted him to. He smiled. He knew just the people to call in order to keep the gravy train moving for everyone. It really paid to have dirt on people. Even the most seemingly insignificant person could come in handy at the right time.

Chapter 4

Two cups of coffee didn't help and couldn't halt the constant yawns that made their way through Karen's mouth. Tired didn't even come close to describing the way she felt. All of her attempts to go back to sleep were interrupted by dreams—dreams about people in the past, dreams about people that reminded her of herself and D-Roc.

And the words… She couldn't get those haunting words out of her head. Voices that sounded different but somehow said the same thing. *We'll be together forever… Our souls are connected, and that will last forever…*

If she didn't have the utmost faith in her own sanity, she might have thought she was going crazy. But as long as the voices stayed in her dreams and didn't start telling her to kill three people or some foolishness like that, she figured she was okay. She was almost tempted to go next door to see Dicey and get that reading she was always trying to tempt her with.

Nah, I don't believe in that woo-woo stuff. It's just crazy dreams. Stress or something like that...

"Good morning, Karen." D-Roc came waltzing in on time with two cups of what looked like far better coffee than the stuff she'd brewed when she came in.

"Morning." She inhaled. It smelled a whole lot better than her coffee, smelled like it would do a much better job at waking her up than the no-name stuff she had.

"You look like a caramel latte kind of girl." He leaned over, handing her the fancy cup of java, and she wondered if there was such a thing as "love at first random act of kindness."

She glanced at him, gave him a slow appraisal and liked what she saw. He was wearing khaki slacks with a short-sleeved red, green and khaki plaid button-up that was unbuttoned with a red T-shirt underneath. He looked good. Really good.

"I had to stop and get some for myself and figured it would be... I mean if you don't like caramel latte, you can have this. It's just plain Jamaica Blue Mountain. I did take a few sips already, but..." he rambled.

She realized that she was looking at him with her slanted-eye incredulous expression, and it probably made him more nervous than she wanted him to feel. The guy had just brought her some delicious pricey coffee after all. Karen reached out and took the latte from his hand.

"Thanks, I really appreciate it."

"Rough night?"

"You could say that. You look like you've had a rough night, too. A little too much partying, huh?"

"No. No partying. Just couldn't sleep. I had some pretty weird dreams, not really nightmares…just weird. The sleep wouldn't come and stay put. I kept waking up. Finally, I just got up and ah…worked on some lyrics. I was suddenly very inspired to write a song."

Hearing him describe almost exactly the same lack-of-sleep night she'd had, Karen felt a slight tremor go down her spine.

"So—" he pulled up a chair and camped in front of her desk before continuing "—what does a brother have to do to get you to give him a chance?"

Talk about loaded questions! It was clear to her the brother had other things on his mind besides community service. Or was that just her wishful thinking?

Nah, brother man had an agenda, a *panties* agenda. She knew a brother on the prowl when she saw one. The only problem was she felt like she wanted to give in to whatever he was gunning for.

She wanted the man.

That was the plain and simple, honest-to-goodness truth.

She let out a short breath and took a sip of her latte. "Why?"

"Why?" he repeated.

"Yeah, why? Why are you so intent on helping out here? As far as rappers go, you certainly don't need to work on your image. You might even have Will Smith beat when it comes to being hip-hop's golden boy. And you put out goody-two-shoes feel-good rap music. No gangsta…no politics…just happy-happy—"

He frowned as he interrupted her. "You sound like you have a problem with music that makes people dance and feel good."

She shrugged. "I don't have a problem with it. It is what it is. It's not my particular vibe. I tend to go toward more conscious stuff, political stuff—old-school Public Enemy, new-school Dead Prez..."

She didn't need to tell him that she also had his CDs in her collection. She certainly didn't need to tell him that she had purchased them, particularly the one with his shirtless muscled torso, strictly for the covers. And she definitely didn't have to tell him that she had jokingly told her girlfriends and Amina that he was fine and he was her future husband and baby daddy whenever they were watching music videos or whenever they went to see one of his films. She shook her head. No, she didn't have to tell him any of that.

"But hey, to each his own... In any case, back to my question. You already have a great public image. Did you do something bad that's about to come out in the papers or something? Did you get a new movie role that has you playing a character that works in a youth center? Why do you want to volunteer here? What's your angle?"

She took a sip of her coffee mostly to calm her nerves. She was already leaning toward just telling him yes, he could volunteer there, but she had to be sure. She didn't want anyone using her kids for a publicity stunt. However, the more she hung around him, the more she started to believe that he wouldn't do that.

He took a deep breath and just stared at her for a moment. His eyes squinted, and he rubbed his temple before exhaling and leaning back. Weariness seemed to overcome him as his shoulders sort of slouched and his face became drawn.

"I grew up not far from here in the Louis H. Pink Houses Projects—Pink Houses. The East New York neighborhood will always be home. But it's been a minute since I've been back. Once I moved my grandmother, aunt and little cousin out of here, there was really no real reason to come back. Plenty of rappers think they can make it big and still hang out in the same spots they used to and end up getting got.

"Plus, I was actually too busy touring and recording to get back much. And once Hollywood came knocking... Anyway, I've always donated money through a foundation I set up. It's anonymous mostly because I never wanted to draw attention to my giving. Like you so eloquently noted, I don't exactly need any help in the *golden-boy goody-two-shoes* department." He smiled.

Heat traveled from her neck to her forehead, and she hoped that her cheeks weren't flaming red. *Contrite* didn't even begin to cover what she was feeling. She took a sip of her coffee and gave him what had to be the most sheepish look in the universe.

He shook his head and chuckled. "Yeah, you should be 'shamed! Dogging a brother like that for being a good guy."

"I wasn't dogging you for being a good guy. I was just stating the facts and trying to figure out why you were so intent on volunteering here."

"Mmm-hmm." His sideways glance was intense. "Anyway, I haven't been back here for a long time. But my little cousin, he couldn't stay away once I moved them out of here. He would come and hang out in these streets as if he didn't have a home. I thought once he started college he would stop. But he didn't. He was still hanging with the same crowd, getting into the same things. And two weeks ago, I buried him because he was in the wrong place at the wrong time. And the only thing I could think about as I dealt with the grief is that I should have spent more time with him. That instead of throwing money at him, I should have been here a little more, taken more of his calls, I should have been there..." He sighed, and she could tell he was regrouping and trying to hold it together.

"I'm so sorry for your loss. The death of a loved one is often hard. But do you really want to volunteer? I'd hate to have you commit to helping out here and—"

"And then drop the ball like I did with Frankie?" The pain in his voice was palpable.

Something in her wanted to soothe the frown on his face. If she was honest, something in her wanted to soothe the pain in his soul. It was almost as if she could feel it, all of his pain and disappointment right there, laid bare for only her. And being in such close proximity to him was *such* a bad idea.

There was something about his scent. And it wasn't just the fresh fragrance of his cologne. No, she could have handled that. It was something uniquely his, something like nutmeg, the air after a summer rain and desire. And smelling him was surely making her stupid, because before she could call it back, she stood, walked over to the front of her desk, stood in front of him and reached out her hand to touch him.

She stroked his cheek, and a tingle traveled from her fingers to her core. "You didn't drop the ball with your cousin. You did the best you could. That's the only thing we can do. I learned that a long time ago." She moved her hand and immediately regretted the move. "You know, volunteering here can't replace your cousin. It won't bring him back."

"But it will help me honor his memory. I realize now that anyone can give money. That's pretty easy when you have a lot of it. But time is something that is so much more valuable. It's precious, because it's the one thing you can't get more of no matter how much money you have. Nothing lasts forever." He paused and shook his head.

He smiled before continuing. "Wow, I just remembered this weird part of my dream. These voices saying something about souls connected and lasting forever or something like that."

Her heart felt like it had stopped. But it couldn't have stopped, because if it had then her eyes wouldn't be bugging and her mouth wouldn't be open and she wouldn't be taking a large, gulping breath. But it felt like it had stopped. How in the world was it possible that Darius had dreams so similar to the ones she'd had?

She opened her mouth and closed it again. She wasn't going to touch it because she didn't believe in that woo-woo stuff, damn it!

"Anyway, I want to give something that is more meaningful. I want to give my time. I know it won't bring my cousin back. I know I'm too late to save him, and that will always hurt my soul. But I can hopefully help others and have an impact on others. And I can learn from this tragedy. I know that. I can learn…"

Listening to the pain in his voice made her chest

feel as if it were cracking under a huge boulder. The pressure was almost unbearable. She knew she had to do something.

"You can volunteer here."

What the hell? Did she just say that?

"On a trial basis. We'll go day by day and see how it works out. But I don't want my center turned into a circus, so keep your entourage or groupies or whatever you call them away."

Are you insane? This man is temptation walking. You need to send him packing! The voice in her head sounded like an alarm clock ringing and fire alarms screeching at the same time. But she wasn't listening to it.

He looked up at her, and even though his eyes were still sad, he smiled. He smiled, and her chest felt suddenly lighter. Then she offered a goofy smile of her own.

"Thanks, Karen. You won't regret it."

"I hope not. Okay, well, I might as well give you a tour and let you know what you'll be doing around here. There's a lot of work to be done. Let's hope you don't have second thoughts once you see how much."

"I'm sure I won't. I want to do this."

She stood up. "Okay. So, during the school year we have several after-school programs running and some skills programs during the day for kids who have been kicked out of school or who have various parole situations—mostly juvenile delinquents who come and get skills training while they look for jobs. In the summer, we run all kinds of enrichment and cultural programs all day and work with anywhere from one hundred to two hundred kids. The summer, as you can see by all the youth in the building today, is a very busy time for us. It's hard to meet the need and demand, and we've had to cut back some programs due to budget constraints. We didn't get a major grant we applied for and the money I had to start with… Well let's just say things are tight right now. That's why, at the end of the day…no matter what I think about the kind of influence you'll be on the youth, I can't turn down the free labor. We need all the help we can get."

He winced and took a sip of his coffee before giving her that intense sideways look of his again. "So you think *I'm* a bad influence?"

The way he phrased the question and the confident tilt of his head told her he could care less what she thought about him. But there was a hint of something else there that she couldn't name or place.

It was that hint that made her want to backtrack and hedge instead of hold her ground. It wasn't his fault the current trend in hip-hop did nothing to motivate the youth. His party-and-dance approach to music and life wasn't bad, per se. It just wasn't political or progressive or relevant to the struggle of their people. But who was she to judge?

Then again, his last album had several of the hottest party anthems of last summer on it. The hooks alone were calls for self-interested, live-and-let-live, fight-for-your-right-to-party nonsense. So she supposed if anyone was at fault it would be him.

"I think you could be a better influence if you put your mind to it. You're positive. You're nice. You're generous. But you're not very political. The kids need to be able to think critically about and deal with all of the stuff that life is throwing at them. Some of these kids, the girls and the boys, are just one good experience away from a lifetime in the correctional system. When they hear your music and the way you glamorize the kind of party and bullshit mentality, let's just say it gives them false ideas about just how invincible they are. So let's just keep it real."

"So I guess you didn't have these kinds of issues with Shemar?"

Unable to help it, Karen almost choked on her caramel latte. The mention of her deceased best friend changed the entire self-righteous tone of her stance and voice. She and Shemar had grown up together, although he was a few years older than her. He'd struggled throughout his life with which path to take. Sometimes his music was uplifting—even revolutionary. But for the most part, he released gangsta-rap lyrics laced with violence and misogyny. And she had named her center for him, because like Darius with his cousin, she needed to do something to uplift the good parts of his memory.

"Shemar and I grew up together, and I was close to him and his family. His death was a loss for me personally and for hip-hop because he never really tapped the potential for positive change that his music could have been."

"But that didn't stop you from taking the money he left you to start this youth center."

Whoa! Well, I guess he told me. She simply nodded her head. "I wanted his legacy to do something positive."

"Really? Then I guess I'm just thinking if you could

cut Shemar some slack, then you could cut me some slack. I'm more than the music I make. And I do positive things with the money I make. I donate money through a foundation I set up to centers just like this. I don't make a big deal out of it, because I don't want to. I make the kind of music I make because it's hot and it sells. I can't help the poor if I'm one of them."

Quoting Jay-Z was not going to make her cut him some slack. The intense tingly feeling she got when he came near? Well, *that* was another story.

His scent seemed to flare even more when he heated up—nutmeg, summer rain and desire. If desire had a smell it would smell like him. Yeah, now she was officially nuts, smelling nutmeg and stuff.

"Let's not talk about Shemar."

He hissed at that. "Fine. But you should know that I'm not damaging the youth. I'm an entertainer. I live an upright life. I try my best to promote a positive lifestyle. But I'm just an entertainer. I make music and movies and try to be a positive role model. At the end of the day, that's all I can do."

"Because of the prison industrial complex, a lot of our kids don't have fathers or mothers at home, and if we had more celebrities who had a political consciousness…" She let out an exasperated breath. "You know what? We can just agree to disagree on this one. I think that as a black man you have an obligation to want to uplift the race and help the youth. But that's neither here nor there. My point is simply that some of the kids are hanging on by a string. They're at crossroads that could mean the difference between life and death. And well, I just want you to keep that in mind when you're interacting with them."

She decided to just continue with the tour and stop trying to argue her political beliefs with him. They were clearly too different to see eye to eye on anything.

Chapter 5

She was the most infuriating, self-righteous, irritating woman he'd ever come in contact with!

And he was totally and completely enthralled with her, captivated to no end. It blew his mind that what she thought of him mattered so much to him.

As much as Darius tried to hold on to his indignation and attitude, there was something about the way her voice cracked when she was speaking. Something about the way he could sense her passion and her distress as she talked about these kids she loved that made him count to ten and calm *way* down. She obviously cared about the kids. That didn't give her the right to blame him for the downfall of society, but he dug her fire. Hell, her fire turned him on.

He smirked. "Fine, I won't encourage any partying or having fun around the kiddies."

She shook her head and laughed, clearly glad for the

olive branch and chance to lighten the mood. "Thank you. So, let's finish this tour of the facilities. It's small, but it's home. You already saw my office and our reception area."

Darius followed her throughout the facilities, halfway listening to what she was saying and thinking about why it bothered him so much that she seemed to have so many problems with him.

Truth be told, he shouldn't even be concerned about what this woman thought. There were plenty of women out there ready, willing and able to take him as he was.

She hadn't had any problems dealing with Shemar, and he was thugged out like nobody's business. That guy had shot at cops, spit at reporters and even done some time in jail. Sure, he'd also made a couple of positive songs and had a revolutionary lineage and pedigree, but he didn't do anything with it when he was alive.

Darius made sure he gave back to the community—at least financially. And now he was giving his time…to *her* center no less. And she still seemed to be wary of him.

He sighed.

None of that really mattered. What really mattered was the fact that Karen Williams seemed to think she was too good for him and he was no better than the crap on the bottom of her shoe. And that wouldn't do at all. He would change her opinion of him if it was the last thing he did.

He watched the gentle sway of her hips in that long, black, crinkled skirt she was wearing. The material and length of the skirt meant he really had to use his imagination to envision what she might look like underneath. Good thing he still had a vivid memory of her curves in the jeans she'd wore the other day. She had on a red, black and green T-shirt with "Dead Prez" on the front and "Get Free or Die Trying" on the back.

He shook his head as he thought about her saying that she liked political rap groups like Dead Prez and Public Enemy. He made it his new mission to make sure that D-Roc became one of her all-time favorite rappers.

"And this is one of the rooms where some of our improvement courses are held. Right now there is a literacy class going on. You'd be surprised how many people make it to high school without knowing how to read and write. And once they get caught up in the system or get kicked out of school, it's hard to get them to see the benefit."

Darius peered through the glass window of the door. There were about five older teens in there and a guy who looked to be about thirty or so. He assumed that the guy writing on the board in an animated manner must have been the instructor.

"That's Tony Marcello. He's really great with the kids. He's one of our best volunteers."

Tony looked up and waved at Karen. When he noticed Darius, Darius saw the glimmer of recognition in the man's eyes. The olive-complexioned man with dark black wavy hair vigorously waved them in then, and Darius caught the brief moment of hesitation followed by a sigh coming from Karen.

"I guess now is as good a time as any to start introducing you to folks, but it's not like you need any introduction."

They walked into the classroom, and the five students immediately started talking at once, asking for autographs and saying they couldn't believe he was really there. Some of them started snapping pictures with their cell phones.

"Stop it. You will not take pictures of Mr. Rollins without his permission. You will respect his privacy and treat him the way you would want to be treated. The first person I find trying to snap a picture of Mr. Rollins while he is here helping us out will be the first person to be shown the door. It won't be tolerated."

Darius had to admit Karen was no-nonsense. She had that stern teacher thing down. He couldn't help but smile.

"It ain't like he really wanna be here anyway. I don't see why we have to respect him. He don't really care 'bout what goes on down here." A tall, skinny young kid named Tyrone twisted his lips to the side as he gave Darius a mean look.

"I do care. And I would be more than happy to take pictures with every single one of you before my time is up. But I won't take pictures with anyone who is not doing what they are supposed to be doing around here." Darius cracked a smile at the kids who seemed excited to see him.

"Man, you act like somebody sweating you for your pictures or something. It ain't even like that," Tyrone snapped.

"I understand that, son. And that's cool. But if there are some young people who want to take a picture with me, then they need to be sure to do what they are supposed to be doing around here." He didn't know how stern he should be with the young man, but he knew for sure that he wasn't about to let him be so blatantly disrespectful.

"Tyrone, you need to watch that tone or you'll be heading home." Karen slanted her eyes menacingly and put her hand on her hips.

Darius could tell that Karen worked well with the kids, and he was suitably impressed. However, he felt that a fine woman like her shouldn't have to put up with knuckleheads like Tyrone.

"Sorry, Ms. Williams, but I'm just saying though…he acting like he all that or we sweatin' him or something," Tyrone hissed.

"That's enough, Tyrone." Karen didn't give an inch.

The boy shrugged and sulked.

Darius could tell Tyrone was torn between continuing his cool pose or straightening up so that he wouldn't further aggravate Karen. Darius kept his gaze focused on the young man. In a lot of ways, Tyrone reminded him of himself when he was a kid. Darius turned to Karen and noted that she had crossed her arms and was tapping her foot. Her eyes never left Tyrone's face.

Finally, Tyrone looked up sheepishly and cracked a half smile at Karen. "Aww, come on, Ms. Williams, you ain't got to put me on blast like that."

"It seems like I do, Tyrone. Are you going to apologize to Mr. Rollins or go home? We don't have all day."

"Man… I'm sorry. I didn't mean no disrespect." The words hardly sounded heartfelt coming from between Tyrone's tightly clenched teeth.

It was all Darius could do not to laugh at the hard-won apology. But he accepted it anyway.

"Okay." Karen gave Tyrone a pointed look. "Mr. Rollins and I are going to finish his tour of all facilities."

"Oh, Ms. Williams, can't he hang out here with us for a little while?" One of the young women batted her eyes as she made the plea.

"Nope! You guys have lots of information to cover. You want to do well on those GED exams, don't you?" Karen flashed a sweet dimpled smile.

Darius waved at the students and teacher as he followed her out of the classroom.

"As you can see, you need to keep a firm balance. The kids will try you if they can." Karen shook her head as she spoke.

"Yeah, I see." Darius nodded.

They toured the rest of the small facilities in relative silence, with Karen just pointing out things.

When they finally returned to her office, she stood in the doorway for a moment before entering.

Darius stared at her, taking in her brown eyes with the most brilliant bronze flecks and her auburn locs with a mixture of bronze, copper and one blond loc. On any other woman he figured the multicolored hair would look crazy. But on Karen, Darius couldn't help but think she personified beauty.

He inhaled. There was something about her scent that seemed to beckon him forward. So he leaned forward.

She backed into the door frame, and a tentative smile crossed her lips. If he didn't know that they'd just taken a tour of the facilities, he would have sworn they had just had a date and he was saying goodbye to her after walking her to her door. He got the sudden urge to kiss her.

"You're beautiful." He had to say it.

"Thank you, Darius. But—"

"Listen, I really don't want to be forward. I really want to take my time, get to know you, court you. All that good stuff… But right now, I need you to move into the office and close the door." He couldn't believe he had just given her those directions, and he could tell she couldn't believe it either.

Her eyes widened, and she hesitated slightly before moving slowly backward.

He followed her lead and closed the door behind them. "I'm going to kiss you." Leaning forward, he covered her lips with his own.

Her mouth opened, and she sighed. Her sweet mouth felt warm and welcoming. It had the taste and feel of the sweetest cotton candy—hot and fresh from Coney Island.

He groaned and groaned again, letting his tongue forge deeply into her mouth, twisting and turning, charting his path.

He allowed his hands to trail her body. She felt so good. Finally, he pulled away and took a deep breath. The strong scent of honey, hibiscus and sweet desire assaulted his nostrils.

"Wh-hy did you do that?" Karen panted.

"Because I couldn't stop myself from doing it. I couldn't help doing it." He leaned forward again and captured her lips. His hands again roamed her luscious body. And again he wondered what he was doing.

What happened to playing it cool and putting his mack down smoothly?

She wrapped her hands around his neck and pulled him close. The soft press of her breasts against his chest made him growl.

He had to have her. He pressed against her, letting her feel his desire for her. He rocked against her V, getting as close as he could get without taking off her clothes and taking her on her desk. He gripped her bottom and lifted her slightly so that he could make better contact. Her hips rocked to meet him. Her pelvis strained to bump against him. He knew that he had to stop, but he couldn't. When she let out a soft shuddering breath and her body shook in his arms, he held her until the shaking stopped.

And then, with everything he had inside of him, he pulled away. Breathing came at great cost, because every ounce of the air was laced with her.

He needed more. He needed her.

"You have to let me take you out to dinner, a movie, something, anything. I need to see you." He needed more than that. But he didn't want to totally throw away his skills. He knew how to woo a woman. And this woman made him want to pull out all the stops.

She was still taking deep breaths and looked up at him with a mixture of shock and awe. She probably couldn't believe that she had had an orgasm standing in the middle of her office. "I don't know, Darius. We should probably keep this professional. You know—"

"I want you. I need you. I can't explain why." He leaned forward and brushed his lips across her forehead. "I think you should let me know what you'd like me to do for the time I'm here today." It was probably best if he got out of her office quick, fast and in a hurry.

"Yeah, right…umm. How about stuffing?"

"Stuffing?" He could think of things he wanted to stuff, all right.

"Yeah. We're having a fundraiser next month for special programs that our grants don't cover, and the invitations have to be stuffed in envelopes. And if you could seal them and get stamps on them that would be a bonus."

He stifled the urge to groan. Boy, this wasn't exactly what he'd signed on for. But he supposed men got into a lot more trouble than stuffing envelopes for women as delectable as Karen.

Sighing, he reluctantly pulled away from her. "Point me in the right direction."

She led him to the small room adjacent from her office, and he did groan when he caught sight of the stacks and stacks of envelopes and cards.

"Oh, it's not that bad. You'll be done in no time. And it's for a worthy cause." She grinned, and her eyes twinkled.

"Okay, but if I knock this all out, you have to have dinner with me tonight."

"You don't get to negotiate. You're on a trial basis here, Mr. Rollins." She smirked.

"Yes. But surely you can see that it would be cruel and unusual punishment for me to have to work here with you even for a couple of hours and not be able to see you, spend time alone with you, get to know you. I just feel like we need to get to know each other better." He was pouring it on thick on purpose. But the funny thing was, he really felt himself moving in the direction of that kind of desperation.

She tapped her finger on her lips in contemplation, and he felt a surge travel through him as he remembered what it felt like to kiss those same lips just a few minutes earlier.

"Okay. I'll go out to dinner with you. We can use the time to talk about the center, and I can answer any other questions you might have."

"All right. However you want it. I better get to stuffing."

"Yeah. You get to stuffing."

He watched her walk back to her office and felt an overwhelming sense of possibility.

Chapter 6

Preparing to leave the center that evening, Karen felt a mixture of excitement and apprehension. She was going to have dinner with Darius. The thought made her insides quiver even as it made her heart pound with anticipation.

She still couldn't believe that he had kissed, fondled, bumped and grinded her into an orgasm as she stood in the middle of her office. But all she could do was thank God that she'd had the common sense to wear a panty liner and bring an extra one with her.

At first, she wanted nothing more than to say yes to his request. She even wanted to go on kissing him in her office. Something inside of her made her feel like his kisses could renew her spirit in very real and substantial ways.

And another part of her—a much smaller part to be sure—whispered she should tread very carefully where the rapper was concerned. Silencing that part seemed oh so easy when his lips melded to hers and his arms held her tight. But in the aftermath, when she had all day to think about all the reasons why she shouldn't get involved with him, well, that was another story.

She locked the door and started to close the gate. Hearing footsteps rushing up behind her, she grasped her key in battle mode between her fingers and turned to find Darius behind her.

"Let me get that for you." Darius reached up and pulled the gate down.

She started to tell him that she'd been locking up the center on her own and closing the gate on her own for the past six years and she didn't need any added testosterone to do so. But then she noticed the bulge in his arm and the pronounced ripple in his chest as he pulled the gate down and the words got stuck in her throat.

Damn, he's fine was all she could think.

"Thanks," was the only word she could mutter as he took the keys from her hands, slightly brushing them. He locked the gate.

"You're welcome," he responded, placing the keys back in her hand. "So, you ready to have a nice quiet dinner and get to know one another?"

She'd never been more ready and so unready for anything in all her life.

"Yeah."

He reached out his hand to her, and she took it without hesitation. What was happening to her?

They walked together in silence toward his double-parked vehicle, and he opened the door for her.

Sliding into the car, she couldn't help but wonder if she should take off running in the other direction. She caught his eye, and the slight glimmer sent a shock through her system.

No, she wasn't going anywhere.

She couldn't.

Smooth soul music played softly in the car. They could have had a conversation over the subtle music, yet they rode the majority of the way in silence.

"This is going to sound corny and probably a lot like I'm trying to run game, but since the moment I laid eyes on you I have felt like I know you from someplace, somewhere. I don't know. It just felt like I already knew you and I had to get to know you all at the same time.... Weird."

Darius's deep voice pulled her out of her reverie. And the nervous chuckle he offered after his rush of words made her heart stop and restart as a warm and tingly calm washed over her body. Was it his voice or his laugh or the sincerity of his jitters that caused her to soften into a puddle so quickly? It had to be the mixture of the three.

She wondered if she should tell him that she felt the same exact way about him, that she felt a large chunk of her soul and spirit reaching and calling out to him.

"I think I know what you mean. It's almost like déjà vu. It's like a part of me recognizes you for some reason I can't name. I mean *logically* I know I don't know you at all, don't know the first thing about you. But I know that the part of myself that is reaching for you won't allow me to just ignore my feelings. It is demanding that I get to know you, even against all my better judgment." Karen let the words rush from her lips in a soft, stilted whisper. She kept her gaze firmly planted on the buildings they passed by.

They had decided to go to a restaurant in her neighborhood, Boerum Hill. The neighborhood had lots of funky shops and ethnic restaurants. Smith Street was popping with nightlife and lots of really cool places to eat.

They were close to the restaurant, and she hoped that they could put the awkward conversation behind them once they arrived.

"So you feel it, too? It's not just me?" Darius pulled up to the restaurant. But they both sat still, each eyeing the other as if trying to figure something out.

She had no idea how much she wanted to own up to any of what she was really feeling. It was crazy, wasn't it? Déjà vu wasn't real. And reincarnation? That was just crazy.

She did *not* know this man from another life. She was probably responding to him that way because she'd seen him so much in films and music videos and heard his music. And he was probably acting that way because of his get-the-panties agenda. Yes, that had to be it.

This was not a woo-woo thing. And even if it were a woo-woo thing, she didn't believe in woo-woo. So there!

"I—I don't know. I mean I feel an attraction." She wasn't about to fully admit to the weird sensations she felt. She didn't think she could explain it even if she wanted to. How did she put something like that into words? Her chest felt as if there was a bongo competition going on inside of it. Clamminess and a hyperawareness that made the hairs stand up on her body seemed to be going on simultaneously. How in the heck did wet stickiness and static friction mix? Wasn't it supposed to be one or the other?

No, there was no putting this feeling into words.

"I feel the attraction, too. And I have to say that I won't be able to just ignore it or walk away from it. So don't ask me to do that." His voice was firm and commanding, and she realized that all that over-the-top testosterone actually made her nipples hard. The wanton little things were actually pebbling up at the sound of his voice!

Who'd've thunk it?

"I just think we need to tread carefully."

"If you're feeling half of what I'm feeling then you know there is no treading carefully."

The waiter came to take their order, and she luckily was able to leave his statement where it was. She had no intention of going there. None whatsoever!

The ambience in the neighborhood Italian restaurant was lovely. Soft music played in the background, and hints of garlic, basil and oregano wafted through the air. There were fine white linen tablecloths on every table, along with candles and fresh flowers. The intimate setting seemed to be made for romance. She'd do well to make it through the dinner without being totally swept off her feet.

Eating should've been a good excuse to break away from the pulsing tension and the surge of energy between them. The awkward conversation had subsided, but not-so-subtle glances of want and need replaced it.

She wondered when she'd forgotten how to swallow.

The food, the wine, none of it went down easily with the pounding in her chest and the dryness of her mouth. And every single time she chanced a glance up from her plate, she met his gaze.

"Why do you keep looking at me?" Her voice came out in a soft lilt that sounded *way* too come-hither for her taste.

His eyes were hooded…seductive…mesmerizing. The realization of what he would probably be able to do to her with just one look almost made her want to drop her fork and jet from the restaurant while she still could.

"You're the most beautiful woman I have ever seen and I really can't—hell, I don't want to take my eyes off you."

Now that has to be game, right?

She pursed her lips and gave him a discerning once-over. If the brother thought she was just another groupie he could try and play with his smooth lines and gobbling gazes then he had another thing coming.

He must have noticed the sudden chill in her expression, but it didn't seem to stop him. "And before you start thinking I'm trying to run game on you to get you souped up, you need to know that I don't have to do all that to get a girl."

How the hell did he know I was thinking that?

"I'm not the average girl. Matter of fact, I'm a woman. I'm certainly not one of your little groupie hoochies. So, don't even try to swell my head. I do feel a connection between us, but I'm not going to let it override my common sense."

"That's cool. I like my woman to be smart and able to keep her head."

His woman? Oh, the brother is really starting to lay it on thick now. Please!

She chanced another quick look at him, and his eyes caught her in his web. Her own eyes widened and she swallowed. She could have sworn she felt a sizzling charge. It came from his baby browns right to her heart and surged directly down to her increasingly aroused core.

He smiled, lessening the magnetism just enough for her to snatch herself back.

"You should finish eating before your food gets cold. But just know I do not see you as a hoochie or a groupie. I see you as a stunning, smart, seductive woman, the most beautiful woman I've ever had the privilege of being around. So don't worry. I'm not trying to play you. I want to get to know you."

He was a rapper *and* an actor. Karen figured he could really fake the sincerity that seemed to pour from him. And if he could then God help her. She wanted to get to know him, too. She wanted to get to know him in more ways than she felt comfortable expressing.

"Excuse us. Are you D-Roc?" Two scantily clad women—one black with a weave down to her butt and one white with blond hair and boobs as big as Dolly Parton's—came up to the table. They spoke the question in unison and seemed to bounce up and down as they talked.

Speaking of hoochies and groupies...

"Oh. My. God! I love your movies, sugar," Dolly, Jr. squealed.

"And I have all your CDs. Your music is amazing! You were *so* robbed at the Grammy's last year. You had the party song of the decade on your last CD. 'It's time to just do it, just go for yours and get stupid.'" Queen of the Weave rapped the hook from one of Darius's songs and did a little dance, dropping it like it was hot in the middle of the restaurant and everything.

Karen could only shake her head in stunned amazement.

Darius was gracious, but she could tell he was more than a little peeved that they didn't respect his privacy. "Good evening, ladies. I'll be glad to sign my autograph for you, if you want it. But as you can see, I'm trying to enjoy a quiet dinner with this lovely lady here, and I don't want to blow my chances at making a good impression on our first date."

The Queen of the Weave and Dolly, Jr. glanced at her as if they'd just realized she was even there, and she could tell what was going through their minds just by the looks on their faces. Their expressions read loud and clear: "You're with her?"

Yes, tramps, he's with me. Now get to stepping. Karen gave the chocolate and vanilla Bobbsey twins her fakest smile.

Darius signed the scrap pieces of paper they dug up. And Karen was even nice enough to take a picture of the three of them with one of their cell phones.

As soon as the women walked off, Darius reached across the table and touched her hand. "Sorry about that. Usually people respect my privacy when I'm out on a date."

"That's okay. You're a big star. It goes with the territory."

"Right, it does. But I just wanted you to know that I would never disrespect or allow anyone else to disrespect you. I'm serious. I want to get to know you."

"Cool, let's just eat and get to know each other, then." Karen thought of the dismissed groupies and smirked. "It's time to just do it, just go for yours and get stupid."

Darius hit her with the most disarming smile she had ever seen, and she had to pause.

He smiled again and nodded, and she wondered why the loud pounding of her heart wouldn't go away.

Chapter 7

Darius could feel the resistance coming off Karen like waves. Each tide struck him and made him intensify his pursuit, like a surfer tackling the ride of his life. And, oddly, that's what it felt like. It felt like his life actually depended on the woman sitting across from him eating her chicken marsala, staring at him only when she thought he wouldn't be looking and getting flustered when he caught her.

He was glad she didn't seem extremely fazed by the two fans that stopped at the table. He didn't want anything getting in the way of his being able to get to know her better.

Then again, he wasn't about to let her slip away with *just* getting to know her. He had never believed in soul mates—or that there was one special person out there for everyone. But Karen Williams could certainly make him a believer. His draw to her was just that strong.

When the waiter came back to see if they wanted dessert, Darius arched his eyebrows in surprise and awe when she ordered the mountain-high chocolate cake. He couldn't remember the last time a date ordered dessert. To be fair, he couldn't remember the last time he took a woman to a nice restaurant and shared a meal. The life of a rap star meant he didn't have to do much wining, dining and wooing. The women sort of just threw themselves at him.

"I know you're not going to be able to eat all that by yourself. So, I won't order any—"

"*No,* my brother. You gotta get your own." She inflected a smooth tone reminiscent of that popular soul music commercial from the late 1980s.

A charge went through him, and for a minute, he saw the woman with the Afro again, holding up a black power fist. She merged so completely with Karen that he couldn't tell them apart. He shook his head.

"Fine, then I'll have a slice of German chocolate cake," Darius said to the waiter.

"Mmm… I was trying to decide between that and the mountain-high chocolate cake." Karen got this yearning expression on her face, and for a minute, he imagined what it would feel like to have her yearning and needful for him instead of cake.

"Well, I won't be stingy like you. You can have a taste of my cake."

Hell, you can have the whole thing for just another kiss from those luscious lips.

She smiled and laughed.

And he could have sworn he heard bells chiming, the kind that led to sweet salvation.

After the meal, he didn't want the evening to end. Sure, he knew he had lots to do, and he should probably be making his way to the studio to record a few tracks so that he kept on time with his release for the following year. But he couldn't bring himself to part with her. He couldn't leave her.

"So, would I seem too forward if I suggested a nightcap at my place?" He hedged slightly, sparing the quickest glance at her and noting the soft squint of suspicion that crossed her face.

"You don't quit, do you? I thought dinner was going to be enough for you and you would back off once I agreed. But you are just determined to keep asking for more, huh? You won't stop until the panties drop, will you?"

His mouth fell open, and he could have sworn he heard his eyes go *ping*—or maybe that was the sound a heart made when it stopped and restarted.

With her left eye slanted slightly and her lips twisted to the side, she appeared to be the picture of seriousness. It was only when she cracked a small smile before bursting into a fit of laughter that he knew for sure she was playing with him.

"Oh, you should see your face! It's priceless."

"You ain't right. You ain't hardly right. Here I am trying to come correct and you clowning a brother. That's not cool."

She laughed even harder, and he tried to hold his own laughter in and keep his facade of indignation.

"Just for that, you need to come on over and have a nightcap. It's the least you could do after hurting my feelings."

"Whatever, *D-Roc!* I'm sure it would take more than my little jokes to hurt your feelings."

"You're right. It would take you turning me down and not spending more time with me this evening. Come on, Karen, let's have a nightcap and keep getting to know one another."

"Um, hello. I have work in the morning and you have—"

"One little nightcap and a couple more hours won't hurt us."

"A couple of hours. Uh-uh. No. See, if I looked up *bad influence* in the dictionary, your smiling, sexy face would…" She stopped before finishing, and the cutest shade of red crossed her light brown face.

He'd never seen a black girl blush like that before. It was as if the subtle red undertones in her skin had the heat turned up a notch and came blazing through. It was sweet and very enticing.

"So you think I'm sexy, huh? She likes me. She really likes me," he teased as he leaned in to capture her lips in a kiss.

It was supposed to just be a peck on the lips. But oh, boy… Once their mouths connected there was no stopping them. His tongue turned into an arrow aiming for parts unknown. Her tongue, way more tentative, made a slow but no less aggressive path into his mouth. And the two dueled and dodged and danced and dined. The only thing they didn't do with that kiss was come up for air until the last possible moment. They pulled away from the embrace clearly dazed but also delighted.

Karen smiled. "I'll tell you what. You can come back to my place. That way when I tell you to get to stepping you can just go. I have a feeling getting you to take me back home from your place tonight would be a big haggling session. And I'm not up for more of your persuasion tonight. So we'll have the nightcap on my turf."

He started to tell her that it really didn't matter where they were—her place or his. He was *always* going to be hustling to spend more time with her. She would have just as hard a time getting him to leave her place as she would have getting him to let her leave his place. Something inside of him kicked and pressed and yearned to make this woman his own. He had a feeling there was nothing he could do to stop it besides get her and keep her.

And that was exactly what he decided he would do.

How in the world did I manage to let him con me into letting him into my home? Karen thought as she prepared two glasses of merlot for them to sip as they continued to get to know one another. Didn't she already know all she needed to know about D-Roc?

She walked out of her galley-style kitchen and into the living room of her one-bedroom apartment. The apartment was small. But what it lacked in size it made up for in amenities. It had all of its original wood, from the floors to the built-in shelves and crown molding. The wonderful mahogany wood had been refinished and made the entire small apartment gleam. Her carefully selected furniture, although sparse, fit in nicely. The huge red fluffy sofa with brown and cream throw pillows and the huge square mahogany coffee table in front of it was the extent of her furniture in the living room. She placed a plush artsy brown rug with flecks of red and cream on the floor along with bigger throw pillows for more seating and so that the huge coffee table could double as a dining space. There wasn't any room for a dining room set.

Darius sat lounging on the red sofa looking a little too smug and comfortable for Karen's taste.

She walked over and handed him his glass.

"Thank you. Come on and sit down."

She sat down, making sure to leave a good amount of space between them. She needed to maintain a sense of calm, had to make sure she kept her head. There was something about Darius and her reaction to him that made her feel as if she were in danger of losing all her senses.

"Why you sitting so far away? Come here, girl."

"Girl?" She let out a nervous chuckle and inched a little farther away. "I don't see any girls here. I'm a woman."

"That you are." Darius slid over until he was right up on her.

Since the arm of the sofa prohibited her from moving any farther, she just sat there.

Resting his arm on the headrest, Darius leaned back and used his other arm to push her back with him. "Don't worry, I'm not gonna bite you…yet."

The image of his perfect white teeth nibbling all over her body made her happy she was sitting down, because her knees started to feel like jelly and heat traveled from her face to her core.

"So tell me more about yourself," he said.

"You tell me about you," she said with a sassy grin.

"Okay, let me see…I'm the best rapper in the world—"

She gave him a teasing smirk. "Oh, now, I don't know about all that. You *a'right*. But you ain't no Nas or nothing. Can't flow like Biggie. Don't have the swagger of Jigga. And you don't have the appeal of 2Pac."

"Aw, you got jokes. You need to take that back. It's not right for a woman to dis her man like that."

"Her man?"

"Yeah, girl. I'm your man. You might not know it yet. And I have a feeling you gonna fight it to the death, but, baby, I'm your man."

Her heart flip-flopped, and she felt her breath sputter. Keeping a cool and calm demeanor seemed like a chore, but she knew she had to portray just that. "I'm not looking for a man right now. And if I were, I'm pretty sure you wouldn't fit the bill."

He leaned forward. "You sure about that?"

She swallowed but remained too pigheaded to do the sensible thing and lean back. No, she had to show him that she wasn't fazed.

Yeah, right.

"I'm positive," she squeaked out. Clearing her throat, she repeated, "I'm *very* positive."

His mouth captured hers, and it felt like someone had opened the gates to passion. She didn't even think of pulling away or breaking the kiss. His mouth tasted too delicious, and her need was too great. It was as if he held all the life-giving essentials her body needed and craved, and she was determined to get each and every one of them from that one kiss.

His tongue played with and tickled the roof of her

mouth, and she allowed her own tongue to trace under his probing tongue.

His hand reached under her blouse, and his strong fingers seemed to stake a claim on each area he touched.

Having no more space to move on the sofa, it became difficult to lean back enough to give him further access, but Karen made do, baring more of her body to his determined touch and powerful hands.

A slow and sexy haze started to form, and she really could no longer fathom not having his lips on hers, not having him explore her body. She wanted more. Desire charged the room. It seemed to be dripping from their very pores.

Reaching upward, she wrapped her hands around his neck and held him close. She heard a sweet, humming sound and realized it was both of them expressing divine pleasure at the connection of their lips.

"I need you." Darius stopped kissing only long enough to utter those words, and his possessive lips wouldn't give her the space to respond. In fact, they kept her very busy.

When he finally pulled away and took a ragged breath, he stared at her for several minutes before saying anything. "I only meant to take one peck of those sweet lips and ended up trying to devour them. What are you doing to me?"

What am I doing to him?

Karen's head spun and her pulse raced. She felt as if someone had placed her in the middle of a marathon and told her to not only run but to win. The urgency she felt whenever she was around Darius seemed to duplicate and multiply whenever he kissed her or touched her.

What is he doing to me would be a better question.

But she had no idea if she was brave enough to stick around and figure out the answer.

"Do you think if we…err…um…had sex, we'd be able to get this out of our systems and put it away?"

Who said that?

Surely that wasn't her voice all breathless and wanton.

His eyes widened and then narrowed in a purely possessive way, aiming right in on her, piercing right through her heart. "No. In fact, I have a feeling that if we have sex it will tie us together even more. I know that once I make love to you that will be it. There won't be any turning back. Hell, girl, after kissing you there is no turning back. I have to make you mine."

Oh, boy. You're in trouble, girl.

"This whole, I'm-your-man-I'm-gonna-make-you-mine kick is interesting, even flattering. But it is *so* not necessary, Darius."

"It's necessary, because I feel like you need to know everything I'm feeling. I've never felt this way before."

"I haven't either," she mumbled.

"I should probably leave while I still can. I'll see you in the morning."

"Bright and early!"

"Yeah."

Why didn't she want him to go? She should have been happy that at least one of them had the common sense to walk away from the situation.

He got up as if it was the last thing he wanted to do, and she followed. As they walked to the front door, she purposely thought about all the reasons why Darius "D-Roc" Rollins was the last guy she should have been getting involved with. None of them seemed pressing enough with him standing so close and the smell of his scent wafting through the air. The name of that stuff *must* have been desire, because it made her want him like nobody's business.

His lips lightly brushed hers one more time before he exited out the door.

Chapter 8

Montgomery, Alabama, 1899

"What are you doing on my father's property, Davey Smith? Shouldn't you be off somewhere corrupting our people, selling that bootleg moonshine in your juke joint and writhing to that sinful stuff you call music?" Karolyn Delaney walked around the other side of the bale of hay, keeping Davey in her sights the entire time.

"When I didn't find you in town today passing out your temperance leaflets and railing against all that I hold dear, I decided to come looking for you. Your fiery passion makes my day," Davey said with a smirk.

"You are the devil himself, Davey Smith! My father heard from one of his friends that you were making it your business to stop by and chat me up every day, and now he's putting a halt to the good work I need to do to

help our people see that alcohol is not the way to social uplift and moral standing and make the government finally outlaw that wretched substance."

"Oh, now, come on, Karo. Baby, how can you know until you've tried it? You won't even step foot inside my place, and I bet you never had a sip of whiskey?"

"If our people put away half of the money they spent in your place and havens of sin like it, they might be able to secure a better future for the children."

"I tell you what, if you stop by my place and try to have some fun, just once, I might consider trying things your way." Davey quickly stepped toward her. Before she could move, he pulled her into his arms.

The kiss that claimed her lips could only be described as magnetic—because she couldn't have pulled away if she wanted to once their lips connected and collided.

She opened her mouth fully and let her tongue dart back and forth tentatively in his sweet, powerful, seductive mouth. She felt his jawline tense as he let out a groan.

"Karo…Karo…baby…" Davey moaned her name as he walked her backward toward the big haystack.

They both hit the hay hard, and Davey continued to stroke her mouth with his tongue as he lifted her long skirt.

She knew what was about to happen and no self-respecting lady, no woman dedicated and devoted to uplift, no person who had taken the clubwoman's oath to better serve her people, would allow herself to be taken that way. No dedicated member of the temperance movement would dare let a juke-joint owner and moonshine maker have his way with her like this!

Yet wasn't that a part of the pull and tug of Davey? The fact that she knew the first time she looked in his daring brown eyes that he would have her here, going against all that she stood for and believed, and that she would want and desire every minute of it.

He pulled down her knickers, and his fingers caressed her womanhood in slow circular movements. No man had ever touched her there, and it was something she always thought she'd save for marriage. But there she was, in the hay, letting a sinning juke-joint man have his way with her.

"Karolyn, I want you so bad, girl. So bad. I have to taste you and see if you're as sweet as I imagined." With those words, he put his mouth on the very spot where his hands had begun their torture.

He sucked and tugged and pulled and nipped. And her hips wriggled and writhed and bucked and lifted. Soon stars formed behind her eyes, and she felt her breath leaving her body in such rapid and sharp intervals that she thought she might be having a heart attack or some other episode.

"Davey! Oh, Davey!"

She really wanted to call on Jesus. But given the fact that she was in a barn on a bed of hay with a man's mouth on her sex, she didn't feel it was quite proper to call on the Lord.

"Karolyn, I love you. I'm going to love you forever. We're going to be together forever." Davey's words came just as the stars started to leave her eyes and the greatest pain she'd ever felt engulfed her. Davey had

entered her sex in on full swoop, breaking past her
shield and causing her to cry out louder than she ever
thought she could.

Oh, shit!

Darius leaped from his bed but not in enough time
to stop the spotting of seed that pushed out of his loins.
The dream he'd had was so vivid that he actually thought
he had just tasted the sweetest honey from a woman
ever and that he'd just been in the most gloriously tight
and delectable sex he'd ever experienced. In the dream,
he'd been squeezed so tight that he couldn't hold back
his come. And the only thing that broke his erotic state
was the piercing scream of the woman, the woman that
must have been a virgin, the woman that for some reason
reminded him of Karen.

He couldn't steady his heartbeat no matter how
hard he tried. He got up from his bed and went into the
bathroom to wash up.

He thought he'd left wet dreams behind in the eighth
grade. And he certainly never would have imagined that
he would start having wet dreams about a woman he
didn't even know living in a time period he clearly had
never lived in. But he felt like he was that man and she
felt like…like everything he knew Karen would feel
like.

Right. Sweet. Oh so good.

He had to do something about the attraction. But
what? He hadn't lied to her when he said that he wanted
her to be his. He just had no idea what that would mean
and how he could mean that when he'd just met her.

Deciding that he couldn't sleep, at least not yet, he

grabbed the guitar that always sat in the corner on a stand in his bedroom. He'd taken a couple of lessons. But for the most part, he'd taught himself how to play. He knew he'd probably never play the guitar in one of his shows. He wasn't Wyclef Jean or Lauryn Hill or anything like that. But he did hope to be able to bring more melody into his music.

He'd been working on a song since the first time he set eyes on Karen. So he figured he might as well work on it some more.

Harlem, New York, 1969

The splendor after making love always made Karla feel as if she and Daniel could withstand anything. With his hands gently caressing her back, everything felt good and right.

And then he'd open his mouth…

"When are you going to get real, and leave those jive-time, wannabe revolutionaries alone? With a sister like you by my side full-time, I feel like I could take on the world." Daniel whispered the words in her ear and followed them with a slow and sensuous lick that caused her to tingle from her neck to her toes.

The cruddy motel room with mirrors on the ceiling and a coin slot attached to the bed to make it bounce and jiggle started to close in on her. But she refused to let the orange, brown and aqua psychedelic designs overwhelm her any more than Daniel's supersmooth rap.

"When are you going to see that the street life isn't

doing anything to help our people and get down with the revolution?"

Karla felt like getting out of bed and leaving the room that Daniel had rented for them. She'd had the conversation with him enough times to know where it would lead. He wasn't ready to leave hustling or even to put his street skills to good use for the revolution. So, by all rights, she shouldn't have even been still messing around with him.

The first thing she learned when she joined the freedom fighters was that sisters had to make brothers accountable by giving up the loving when they were on the job and holding back when they weren't. If Daniel wasn't going to join the struggle, then she shouldn't have been sleeping with him. Period. Doing so was being counter-revolutionary.

But the brother was fine. All six-plus-feet of his muscled frame, and even his perfectly picked Afro, had a way of making a sister want to holler with just one look. And hustler that he was, he knew how to work his big brown eyes and sexy dimpled smile so that it went hand in hand with his hundred-dollar rap.

Honestly, once he stepped to her looking all good, dressed to woo and wow, there really wasn't much she could have done not to drop the panties. And once he laid it down, well...he made it hard for her to keep turning him away. So she always found her way back. She just kept telling herself that this time was the last time. She wouldn't continue to let him make love to her if he didn't show that he was down for the people, down for revolution. But she knew it was a lie. This man, so *different from her in so many ways, was the other half of her soul. She'd always come back.*

She felt his growing love swelling and pressing next to her skin. Everything inside of her told her he was the one. Straddling him, she slowly let her tongue trail his sweat-soaked chest. She knew she loved the man. Rising, she centered her sex on his and worked her muscles seductively on the way down.

"Mmm...yeah, baby. That's what I like. That's what I need. Come on and stay with me, baby. Stay with me, and it can be you and me against the world." Daniel arched his back and moaned as he murmured his seductive words.

Adding a bounce to each swivel of her hips, Karla rode Daniel as if her life depended on it.

"You could leave that counter-revolutionary lifestyle you're leading and join us." She leaned down and captured his lips in a soft, pecking kiss before continuing. "I won't be able to see you anymore if you don't. This will have to be our last time together. You don't want that, do you?"

"I told you not to use our relationship as some sort of bargaining tool." Daniel's gaze became heated and angry as he sat up and flipped her over on her back. Still inside of her, he lifted her legs to his shoulders and pushed forward.

Each thrust of his hips set jolts of pleasure to her core and pain to her heart. She could tell by looking at him that he wasn't going to do the right thing and join the revolution.

"All that pussy power crap those tired revolutionary brothers spouting is just so they can get in your pants."

He thrust his hips forward with a vigorously seductive swivel, touching places inside of her that she didn't even know could be touched. "No man is going to let a woman dictate how he lives and dies based on what's between her legs."

Closing her eyes briefly and savoring the tingles that shot from her core to the tips of her toes, she swallowed back a moan. "Well, crap or no crap, I can't keep doing this. I'm living for the people. We can't stay together unevenly yoked."

Daniel laughed at that and brought his mouth down to her nipple. He thrust his hips forward in quick succession as he suckled. An orgasm shot through her that made her back leap from the bed and her inner thighs quiver. She had to close her eyes again so that they wouldn't cross. When she opened them, Daniel's glare was on her.

"'Unevenly yoked'? You ain't saved, and the revolution sure as hell ain't no religion. You gonna have to decide once and for all. Because now...I'm thinking I don't want my lady hanging around a bunch of so-called revolutionaries using their foolish ideas to get in her pants. So you decide. Will it be me or the revolution?"

Daniel moved in and out of her, faster and harder. Her heart began to beat wildly, and her soul began to ache uncontrollably. Just as they both reached their peak and found completion, Daniel fell on top of her. He kissed her passionately and held her close.

"I do love you, Daniel. I always will. But if I have to choose, then my choice will always be the people and freedom. If you can't join the fight, then I might as well

leave now." Pressing her hands against his chest, she moved to leave.

He held her tightly and flashed that sly grin that always tugged at her heart and melted her insides. "No. You're not leaving me, girl. And I ain't leaving you. This is forever. You and me. Forever. I'm your man."

"Forever…you and me…forever." Karen rolled over from her restless slumber with her hands wrapped around herself so tightly she could hardly breathe.

Her panties were wet, and her entire body shook with the aftermath of lovemaking so passionate she could almost still feel him. When had her dreams become so vivid? And why did the people in her dream feel like her and Darius? She had had dreams in which she felt like herself but didn't recognize or look like herself. But this felt like straight up recalling another lifetime, like remembering *herself* in another lifetime.

Running her hand across her face, she took slow, halting breaths.

When the deep inhalations didn't seem to be doing any good, she got up on her shaky feet and walked to her kitchen. She figured a glass of water or a cup of tea might help. But then she noticed the bottle of wine that she'd opened when Darius was there and opted for a glass of that instead.

She took the glass back to her bedroom and sat down. Taking slow sips, she reached for the leather-bound journal that she'd found while cleaning out Amina's attic.

Opening the yellowing, aged pages, she turned to and found exactly what she'd been afraid she'd find—entries from Karolyn D. She'd been a clubwoman doing good work on temperance and uplift in the community and then she met a juke-joint owner named Davey. There were also entries from Karla, Amina's sister the black revolutionary, telling all about her relationship with Daniel the street hustler. She tried to think about what all those relationships had in common and what they could possibly have to do with what she was feeling about Darius.

Karen sighed, took a sip from the wine and set it back down on her nightstand before grabbing a pen. Turning to the last entry in the journal, dated November 15, 1970, Karen began to write on the next empty page. She had no idea what possessed her to write in the journal. She just felt a pressing feeling in her heart.

As the words began to bleed onto the page, she felt the pressing ease just a bit. What she wrote surprised her more in some ways and seemed like a given in others.

Only two days ago, he walked into my youth center. I have no idea how I'm going to be able to resist him or even if I should. All I know for sure is that Darius "D-Roc" Rollins is doing something to me. My soul seems to recognize him and wants him even though my mind is reeling and railing against the very thought. I couldn't think of two more diametrically opposed individuals. My life mission is about helping the youth. His music and message seem to be all about partying and having fun. I know all of this and still I'm drawn to him. I'm as drawn to him as I am to this journal, a journal filled with the stories of women who have loved men they seemed to be at odds with philosophically. The

part of me that is reaching for Darius, for his heart and soul, is also telling me to work out my feelings through words here in this book. So I guess I just write and hope and pray...
Until next time,
Love and peace,
Karen W

Chapter 9

Getting up the next morning and heading into the center was difficult to say the least. Karen didn't know how she could continue to face Darius with all the dreams she'd been having. Even though she told herself that the dreams weren't about him—*weren't about them*—something deep in her spirit said they were. Passing Dicey's Divine Intuition, she made a mental note to go in and visit Dicey for a reading. The woman had been trying to get her in there for the longest time. Maybe that would help her figure this out. Maybe she needed her aura checked or some woo-woo stuff like that.

She wasn't the type to take those kinds of things too seriously. But then she'd never had strangers who seemed familiar invading her dreams before either.

As soon as she walked up to her building, Darius got out of his car and walked over carrying coffee.

She smiled at him. "You're early today."

"I couldn't wait to see you again."

She couldn't help staring at him to see if she could tell if he was being sincere or running game. His chocolate-drop eyes showed a hint of tiredness, but they also seemed to shine true. Quickly turning away, she walked back toward her office with him right on her heels.

"I brought you another caramel latte." He handed her the drink and sat down. He narrowed his eyes and leaned forward. "Here's the thing. I have been having a hell of a hard time sleeping since I met you. You are so deep in my system that I'm starting to have a hard time distinguishing between up and down, right and wrong. Hell, the only reason I can manage to get up in the morning is because I want to see you. And you might think a brother is running game and not believe a word I'm saying to you. But I'm being more real than makes sense to me right now because I just met you."

He took a deep breath and shook his head. "Tell me you feel me, girl."

Oh, she felt him all right. But how did she tell him that she'd been having weird dreams that woke her up, dreams about people she didn't know, but that she knew so well.

How did she tell a man that she just met a few days ago that she saw lifetimes, futures, hopes, dreams and everything in between when she looked into his eyes?

You don't tell him that, foolish girl! the rational side of her seemed to scream.

"Darius—I really don't know what to say. We just met. I barely know you, really. I think we're already moving way too fast. Things feel so intense, and we haven't even done anything but talk and kiss—you know?"

Just that and you gave me a couple of mind-blowing orgasms without even taking off my clothes. But really what is a couple of orgasms between virtual strangers?

She sighed. "I feel like if we don't put on the brakes we are liable to combust, go up in flames and explode, you know?"

"And I feel like if we don't do something about this attraction, if we don't act, we will for sure ignite and burst. I have a feeling it could be... I'm not sounding very smooth right now. This is not cool at all. But I'm gonna be real with you because you need to understand this. Karen, I know in my gut that I'm meant to be your man. I have got to have you. I'm staking my claim, girl. You're mine."

He got up from his seat. "I'll be around for a couple of hours today. But, I'll be back tonight to pick you up."

"You'll be back tonight. Who said anything about—"

"Karen, don't ask me how I know this, but you and I are destiny, baby. Like I told you the other night, I'm your man. See ya later."

And he trotted off like he'd just proclaimed that the sky was blue or some other real and verifiable thing that could easily and readily be shown and proved. His confidence. His stance. His swagger. They all seemed to scream, "I'm a cocky and arrogant man, but I got you, baby. You're mine."

For all her womanist leanings, she could not find it in herself to refute him. Everything inside of her yearned to make his words come true. What was she going to do?

Once the day got started, there was really no time to reflect, ponder and daydream about her intensely growing feelings for the rapper and actor. She had a center to run.

She was impressed, though, with how easily Darius seemed to fit in to the flow of things at the center. Just like when he stuffed envelopes the other day, he did the tasks she asked of him without complaint. He took initiative when appropriate and did some things without having to be told.

More importantly, he was excellent with the youths. She'd walked up on him several times that day having conversations with groups of students about the importance of education and hard work. They were the things she drilled into them every day, but he made it seem fun, almost glamorous. The first time she had eased up on him and two of the boys, she'd thought she was going to have to break up some kind of lurid discussion, they had been laughing so hard. But what she found were two of her more difficult young men totally enthralled with Darius's story of being in community college and working full-time to pay for his demo.

After he put in several hours, he left to go and check on his grandmother and aunt. But he'd certainly left an impression on the youths. And if she were honest, he had left an impression on her, as well.

After taking her quick and sufficient—but not necessarily tasty—low-calorie frozen meal out of the microwave, she went to her office for a quick bite before finishing her tasks for the day. Just as she was about to put the first spoonful of the Latin-inspired chicken-and-rice dish in her mouth, her phone rang.

"Shemar Sunyetta Youth Center, this is Karen Williams speaking."

"Ms. Williams, this is Cullen Stamps, D-Roc's manager—"

"Darius has left for the day, Mr. Stamps. He went to check on his relatives. I'm sure you might be able to reach him on his cell."

"I'm not calling to speak to him. I'm calling to speak to you, Ms. Williams. I think we may have gotten off on the wrong foot. It's not that I don't appreciate the work you're doing with the youth. I suppose someone has to do it. My point is that D-Roc doesn't have the time, and I need to know how much it will take for you to put an end to this trial-basis bullshit and let him go so that he can get back in the studio."

Shocked, Karen's mouth fell open. For the first time in her life, she found herself speechless. That hardly ever happened to her.

"I've done my research on you, *Ms. Williams*." The way he said *Ms. Williams* sounded as if he were saying *common street whore* instead. "I know you can be bought. So how much is it going to cost me?"

Is this pencil-pushing pimp parading as a manager calling me a whore?

The outrage she felt almost refused to be contained. She took deep, calming breaths and tried to uncross her eyes. They seemed to have gotten stuck. She shook her head and took another breath.

"Mr. Stamps, I don't know what you think you've heard about me. And I really don't know what could have given you the idea that you could continue to insult me and I'd continue to give you a pass—" she paused, breathed in deeply and let it back out "—but I will give you the benefit of the doubt this time. The fact of the matter is no matter what you've heard or what you think you know about me, you don't know me!"

She stopped and took several more calming breaths. Professionalism sucked in cases like this. There were some people in the world that deserved to be blacked out on, some people who deserved a real good cussing out. Cullen Stamps was one of them. She wondered if he was any relation to her aura-reading neighbor, Dicey "Divine" Stamps. If he was, they were about as different as night and day.

"I know you started your little center with the large sum of money your dead friend, Shemar Sunyetta, left you. I know that he also gave you money while you were attending Brooklyn College. Did his funds keep you off the pole? Do you see D-Roc as a way to replace the Shemar money train you got so used to *riding?* You can forget about it. He'll see you for what you are soon. I'll make sure of it. So why don't you do us all a favor and take the money I'm offering you to let him go? Now!"

That was it. Disrespecting her, disrespecting her best friend's memory, he had to be told off.

Professionalism be damned!

She was a Brooklyn girl at heart, and that would *never* change.

No! She would not let this idiot take her control. She was a strong, poised, professional black woman. And how would she be able to lecture to her youth about maintaining control if she let this fool get to her?

"Mr. Stamps, your client has made a decision to devote some time to our center, and we appreciate all the help we can get. I'm not going to turn his generous offer down. Money is something we can always find. But folks willing to devote the precious commodity of time? Not so much. Mr. Rollins is a grown man who has made a decision to give back. *You* work for him. I suggest you respect your client's decision."

"Look, you little bitch—"

"Please, Mr. Stamps, I know the concept of respect might be a little foreign to you, but you should know I *won't* be called a bitch. So, I'm going to do us both a favor and end this call now. Do not call me again! If you want Mr. Rollins to stop volunteering, then you should speak to him about that." She hung up the phone because she was tempted to throw in a couple of derogatory words for good measure. A girl could only hold back so much until she burst.

She rubbed her temple and wondered just how much trouble Mr. Stamps was going to be.

Her stomach was still growling, and she realized that she needed something more than the little—now cold—microwave rice dish in front of her. In fact, it didn't look very appetizing at all now that it was cold. A nice veggie sub from the bodega on the corner would be much more satisfying. She told her staff she was running out to grab a bite and planned to bring her sandwich back to the office to eat while she worked. She had grant applications and proposals to finish, and the deadlines were creeping up on her like crazy.

Just as Karen walked back to the center, Dicey came walking out of Divine Intuition.

"I see you've met him," Dicey offered with a knowing grin.

"Met who?"

"Your other half, your soul mate, dear one."

"Yeah, right, Dicey." Karen gave an uneasy laugh and shrugged her shoulders.

"You don't have to confirm or deny anything to me, dear one. I can see it all in your aura. You and he have done this dance many times before and you'll no doubt be doing it many more times to come. The only question is if you will make the most use of your time together this time. How much time will you waste?" Dicey patted her forefinger on her chin as if in deep contemplation.

Tired of Dicey's little insinuations, Karen gave the woman a piercing glare. "Do you think you know something about me?"

"I think I could tell you a whole lot and save you a lot of time and energy if you were brave enough to sit for one reading." Dicey's voice held its normal enticing tone, but this time it seemed like it was more powerful.

"Dicey—" Karen started to go with her normal rejection in spite of how much she wanted to go get a reading.

"Divine," Dicey corrected.

Karen bit back her retort that Divine wasn't hardly Dicey's real name. However, she realized that Dicey probably wasn't her real name either.

What the hell was her real name?

Karen let out an exasperated sigh. "*Divine,* I already told you I don't believe in all that woo-woo stuff. Just me, my self-determination, will, drive and a little *Je-sus* is all I need."

"Hmm…yes…Jesus… 'I turned myself into myself and was Jesus. Men intone my loving name.'" Dicey smiled when she saw Karen looking at her strangely. "Just a little of Nikki Giovanni's 'Ego Tripping.' I've always loved that poem. It's such an homage to the divine in all black women, don't you think?"

"Yes. It's one of my favorite poems." Karen paused and then finished the line from the poem that Dicey started. "All praises all praises. I am the one who would save."

"Yes, dear one. I'll tell you what, since we both have a fondness for the warrior sister poets of the 1970s, I'll offer this reading for free. If you feel like leaving a tip after you hear what I have to say, fine."

Man, she is really making it hard to say no today. Or was it that Karen really wanted to get a better sense of what was going on with Darius?

"I don't have long. Maybe another—"

"It won't take long. Come on in." Dicey held open her door and waved Karen in.

Karen walked into the cozy storefront and was pleasantly surprised. She didn't know what she had been expecting. Skulls? Bones? Black? Crystal balls? Tarot cards? She certainly wasn't expecting the warm, earth-toned furnishings accented with splashes of jewel tones. The combination of the rusts, browns, creams and mahogany were nicely highlighted with hints of emerald-green, ruby-red and gold. The chairs were oddly placed, but each one was overstuffed and comfy. The throw rugs were placed haphazardly, but each one was plush and buoyant.

She watched as Dicey lit up various candles about the room.

"Pick a seat wherever you feel the most comfortable, dear one, wherever the energy is the most productive for you."

Karen sat down in a soft cream chair that felt like a cloud. The extra green and gold throw pillows added to the overly plush feel of the chair.

Dicey finished lighting the candles, and then she sat down in the brown-and-mahogany chair across from Karen. She placed the ruby-red chenille throw across her lap and reached for Karen's hand.

Karen held her hand out and gave a nervous chuckle. "What, no crystal ball?"

"If you're not going to take this seriously, Karen—"

"Okay. Okay. I'm just joking." She opened her hands palm side up and took a deep breath.

The truth was Dicey had been saying things that struck way too close to home. And between Dicey and that journal, D-Roc and the dreams, she knew she needed answers from somewhere. The journal just made her have more questions, because she didn't want to believe that she was really somehow spiritually connected to all those women. Because if she believed that then she had to believe the other part of it, that Darius was her soul mate. Dicey just might be her best hope at sanity and reason.

Imagine that.

Dicey didn't look at her hands at all. She looked right into her eyes and seemed to peer right into her very soul.

"You have old souls, you and he. And you've been very lucky to keep finding each other across time. You've always seemed to represent opposite paths. But you work best when you're open and willing to learn from one another. You're all about the people, doing what you can for the uplift and the cause of freedom. You've been a race woman, a black revolutionary. You've even been an abolitionist helping folks steal away to freedom on the Underground Railroad. Your souls go back very closely to the beginnings of time."

Ok-ay. Wha-ev-er. The beginnings of time? Ye-ah ri-ght. Karen was about to laugh, but a strange feeling came over her. Karen clutched her hands on her lap as the eerie chill coursed through her body.

"I'm starting to think you had something to do with that journal, Dicey. Did Amina put you up to this?"

"I didn't have anything to do with you getting the journal this time, and please call me Divine, dear one. As I was saying, the two of you seem to be opposites. But that's only to people who aren't looking carefully, who aren't paying attention. The two of you *cannot* be the ones who aren't paying attention." Dicey grasped her hands and held them tightly when she said *cannot,* as if she needed to stress that more than words would allow her.

Karen slanted her eye. "Ri-ght. Ok-ay."

"So skeptical. So serious." Dicey let out an amused chuckle. It was almost as if she were pooh-poohing Karen's silliness or something.

Karen frowned because she knew the woo-woo lady couldn't possibly be pooh-poohing her. "So, let's say I buy everything you're saying. And let's say Darius and I are these two souls who are for some reason continuing to meet up and hook up or whatever across time. Why? What could possibly be the reason for it?"

"You mean besides the fact that he's your soul mate, dear one?" Dicey arched her eyebrow and twisted her lips.

"A reason that makes *rational* sense, not that I don't believe in soul mates or anything…but, come on."

"Well, sometimes souls are destined to connect and reconnect until they get it right. You know, work out all the kinks that stopped them from connecting more fully in past lives. Some people are destined to repeat their lives until they learn the lessons they are supposed to learn. Could be you're just doomed to do it till you get it right. Sometimes souls have things to learn, and it takes them a little longer than one lifetime to learn it. Could be you have to learn how to do something that you maybe didn't do in your past life. Maybe he has to learn how to devote his time to a righteous cause, and maybe you need to learn how to lighten up, relax and have fun. Or it could be no rhyme or reason to it at all, dear one. It could very well be that you are lucky enough to keep meeting up with the other half of your soul. Why not just enjoy it?"

Dicey closed her eyes and tilted her head back. "If you really need to rationalize it, then any one of those could be the case or none of them at all. Does it matter when you think about how your heart feels when he's around? Your entire aura is telling me that it doesn't. Don't ignore that."

Karen looked at her watch before opening her purse. "Well, I have to get back to the center. Those grant applications aren't going to write themselves. How much do you normally charge for these readings?"

"This one was on the house, and because I'm feeling nice, I'll throw in one more thing. If he is your soul mate, then he is literally the other half of you. The two of you complete each other, and your differences can only enhance and enrich one another *and* the relationship. You have to embrace it for what it is or risk losing your shot at happiness this lifetime. There will be plenty of people working to make the two of you fail. You don't need to be in on it with them."

Ri-ght. Ok-ay. "Well, I'll take all of that into consideration. Thanks for the advice, Divine." Karen got up, shook her head and chuckled softly as she started walking out. Dicey "Divine" Stamps had given her more than enough to think about, that was for sure. Thinking of Dicey's full name made her remember Darius's creepy manager.

"Oh, by the way, are you related to a Cullen Stamps?"

Dicey twisted up her lips, and it looked like she had tasted something sour. "Yes, he's my little brother, why?"

"He's Darius's manager and a really unpleasant person."

"Unfortunately he's always been unpleasant, and he always will be. He could never find our father's favor, and goodness knows he's been jealous of me for more years than I can count. He doesn't like anyone happy. So, I'd watch out for him if I were you."

Karen pursed her lips as she studied Dicey carefully. Cullen being related to Dicey was just one coincidence too many. She decided then and there to take everything Dicey said with a grain of salt. For all she knew, Dicey was probably in cahoots with her brother. She had no idea what they hoped to gain by getting her to believe that Darius was her soul mate. And there was also the fact that Dicey and Cullen seemed to have opposite and competing agendas when it came to her and Darius. But until she figured it all out, she would just place Dicey's advice in the back of her mind.

"I'll certainly watch out for him." *And you, too.* "You never know who you can trust these days, that's for sure." With those words, Karen left Divine Intuition and went back to the center to wolf down her veggie sub and finish her grant proposals.

Cullen fumed and sulked for a full six minutes after getting off the phone with Karen. He wasn't going to let *her* get in the way of his plans. And he wasn't going to lose again.

Not this time…

He had too much riding on Darius doing exactly what he wanted him to do.

He picked up the phone and made some phone calls to check the progress on his demands from a few days ago. He made one call to the person who had given him all that useful information about Karen and her center, one to the person who could help him get Darius back in line and another to his two aces in the hole.

Karen and Darius would be over before they even began if he had anything to do with it.

Chapter 10

"Hey, son. I'm so glad you stopped by. I made your favorite—sweet potato pie." His grandmother gave him a warm and loving embrace that made him wish he made it home to visit more often. "Come on back in the kitchen. I'll cut you a big slice."

He followed his grandmother back into the kitchen. Aunt Janice was sitting at the large cherrywood kitchen table smoking a cigarette and wearing her typical angry-at-the-world expression.

"Hey, Janice." He walked over and gave her a hug even though he really didn't want to get any smoke on him.

The smell of cigarettes made him want to retch. He hated that Janice essentially had the home he purchased for his grandmother smelling like an ashtray.

The yellow-and-white kitchen had cherrywood cabinets and stainless-steel appliances. Everything was top of the line. He'd made sure that the decorator he hired understood that he'd wanted only the best for his family. The room should have been bright, cheery and airy. But with Janice's chain-smoking, everything seemed to be tinged with a dull gray blight.

Janice gave him a half-pat-on-the-back hug and didn't even bother to get up out of her seat.

"Janice, why don't you put that cancer stick out? You know the boy never liked the smell of those things." His grandmother waved her hand back and forth as she frowned. She went over to the stove and cut him a big slice of sweet potato pie.

When she sat next to him, she smiled and rubbed his shoulder.

Janice twisted up her lips and cut her eyes at her mother and Darius. "He don't live here. Why should I have to stop doing what I do all the time just because he decides to bless us with his presence? Please! He needs to go the hell back to Hollywood and leave us alone." She blew out an exaggerated ring of smoke and cut her eyes again.

"It's okay, Grandma. Janice is going to be Janice, regardless of how many folks she kills with her second-hand smoke." He took a bite of the pie. The burst of cinnamon and vanilla hit him right away as he savored the layers of flavor in the filling and the perfectly flaky crust. The only thing that ruined the sensory experience of eating the pie was the nicotine-and-menthol smell wafting through the air.

"This is the best, Grandma. You outdid yourself as usual. You know I'm gonna have to get another two or three more slices of this." He winked at her, and she grinned.

"Boy, you know when you're in town I always make an extra pie. You can take it with you. I forgot that Frankie wasn't here…so Janice and I can have the extra pie I made for him. You eat as much as you want."

Janice sucked her teeth in disgust and jumped up from the table. "What you doing here anyway? Thought you said you was going to be volunteering your time in the hood to help other kids the way you should have been there to help Frankie? You might as well go back to Hollywood since you ain't there for those kids either."

Darius counted to ten in his head before looking up from his plate. "I am. I'm volunteering at the Shemar Sunyetta Youth Center. I just wanted to take some time to check on you two and see how you're holding up."

"Mmm-hmm." Janice inhaled on her cigarette and exhaled slowly, all the while looking at him through a squinted eye glare.

"Shemar Sunyetta? Seems like I've heard of that name before…on the news. He was a rapper, too, like you, right? He was murdered a few years ago." His grandmother's forehead crinkled in contemplation.

"He was a better rapper than Darius, Mama. Shemar had flava *and* he was fine," Janice said with a smirk. "I think I remember hearing something about some girl he left a bunch a money to using it to start a center in his honor. She must be one simple chick. I wouldn't have used that money for no damn youth center."

"Well, it's a good thing not everyone is like you, Janice. From what I've seen so far, the center does good work. And Karen is a very dedicated and committed sista. She's down for the cause and working for the people. And there isn't one simple thing about her." He realized that he maybe had a little too much agitation in his voice.

"Mmm-hmm." Janice eyed him suspiciously.

"Anyway, I'm learning a lot about the center and the work she's doing, and I plan to donate some money, as well. It's important work, and she can use all the help she can get." He eyed Janice's suspicious glare and found his neck heating up. He felt the need to prove her wrong. "And I also plan on going back to personally volunteer there whenever I get a break between movies and the studio." *Take that, Janice!*

Janice inhaled on her cigarette and exhaled slowly and dramatically. *"Ye-ah. Wh-at-ev-er."* She smirked. "What did this community center chick do with all that money Shemar Sunyetta left her? Were they a couple or something? She must be a good-ass chicken-head if she got all y'all rapper types throwing money at her."

"Janice!" His grandmother waved her hand at his aunt.

If only that would shut her up, but Darius knew that it would take more than shock or outrage from his grandmother to shut his aunt up.

"Anyway, Grandma, I'll be back later this week to check on y'all." He got up. As much as he wanted to be there for them, his aunt's usual nasty mood was extra since Frankie's death and he just didn't have the patience. He'd end up saying things he couldn't take back if he stayed.

His grandmother got up and wrapped one of the sweet potato pies in aluminum foil. "That should hold up for you. I'm cooking all your favorites for dinner on Sunday. You coming to church with me, right? Pastor would love to see you…"

"*Whatever!* Mama, I don't know why you bother with that. That boy ain't going to no church. I bet he won't even stick around a full month. Volunteering my ass!" Janice tapped her acrylic nails on the kitchen table and shook her head so that her long, flowing weave bounced around, all the while puffing away on her cigarette.

He glared at his aunt and gave his grandmother a peck on the cheek. *Yep, it is time to go.* "I'll see you on Sunday, Grandma. I'll come pick you up for church. See you later, Janice."

He left the house earlier than he had intended, but with his sanity intact. He decided to pay Cullen a visit just to touch base with his manager since he had some time before he had to go back and pick up Karen for their date.

Cullen was out in the front of his office yelling at the receptionist and appeared to be in an even grumpier mood than usual. He looked up when Darius walked in and shook his head. "So the little bitch gave you my message?"

Darius frowned and looked behind him to see who Cullen was talking to. Seeing no one behind him, he slanted his eye questioningly. "What the hell are you talking about, Cullen?"

"The community center bitch. I called the place to speak to you and the little—"

"Are you talking about Karen?" He cut Cullen off, and the heat steadily rose from his chest to his forehead and his eyes narrowed and glared. "Her name is Karen, and I'd appreciate it if you never called her out of her name again."

"What the hell are you getting all touchy for? What? I can't call a bitch a bitch because I'm not a rapper?" Cullen laughed at his own joke.

"You can't call her out of her name if you want to continue to do business with me. She's a special woman who works hard and is devoted to a positive cause. Show some respect!"

Cullen rolled his eyes. "Fine. Whatever. Listen, you need to get back in the studio like yesterday. You don't have that much time before you have to start filming again. There's still a lot of work to be done. And maybe this isn't the best time for you to be volunteering at some center. Do us all a favor and write a check."

"This is important to me, and I'm doing it." He hoped the firmness and finality in his tone was enough to get Cullen to back off.

"Listen, I didn't want to say anything about this. But you're leaving me no choice." Cullen sighed and ran his hand across his closely cropped hair. "I did some background checking on this woman, and she has a history of messing around with men with money. In fact, the money she used to start her center came from another popular rapper who was murdered—Shemar Sunyetta."

"So what? He was her best friend. They grew up together—"

"He left her a pretty sizable sum of money, and a portion of his royalties go to her, as well. She could be looking for the next big paycheck."

"Look, I'm not going to say this again. If you can't

respect Karen, then you need to just keep her name out of your mouth. I'm not having this discussion with you. I'm volunteering at her center, and that's final." Darius narrowed his eyes and clenched his teeth as he bit out his words. Cullen might be his manager, but he would not tolerate anyone disrespecting Karen. It went against every fiber in his being.

Cullen's eyes flickered with slight irritation. Darius made sure he held Cullen's gaze.

"Fine. Whatever. If you want to be hardheaded and let this chick stick you for all you're worth—"

"No one is sticking me for anything. Change the subject, Cullen! As a matter of fact, let's just call this a wrap. I'll be in touch when I'm ready to hit the studio." He got up and walked out of Cullen's office.

It felt good.

He still had about an hour to kill before it was time to pick up Karen. He'd been thinking about her all day. By the time he drove there from Cullen's office in New York traffic, he'd just about make it.

Waiting outside of the center for Karen felt like waiting for *The Source* magazine reviews to come out just after an album dropped. No matter how much Darius told himself he couldn't care less what people had to say, he couldn't quite sit right until he saw the five mics and the glowing review. With Karen, heck, he'd never felt more open and anxious. He wanted the woman in a bad way.

She was five minutes late. Did that mean something like she wasn't coming out? Or maybe she just wasn't feeling him?

Nah, he had kissed her, and he knew she was feeling him. She might be trying to run from it. She might not want to own it. But she felt him.

He glanced at the door and willed it to open, willed her to come walking out and lock up.

The door remained shut.

He pulled in to a spot and parked, since he'd been double-parked. He shut off the car and got out. Just as he walked around the car and turned on the alarm, she came walking out.

"Hey," she mumbled as she juggled her bag and tried to lock up.

Darius rushed over and took the bag from her hand. "I thought you weren't gonna come out."

"Why would you think that?"

"I don't know. I just…I don't know. Just nerves, I guess."

"What do you have to be nervous about?"

"Nothing now, I guess."

They walked to the car, and he opened the door for her to get in before getting in himself. "So, where do you want to go?" he asked once he got in the car.

"Wherever you want to take me." She let her words trail off, and he could think of only one place he wanted to take her at that moment: his house. His bedroom, to be exact.

Chapter 11

"Where Brooklyn at? Where Brooklyn at?" The loud bumping base of the music was matched only by the deejay hyping up the crowd in the crowded nightclub. All the deejay had to do was ask the question and the crowd was more than willing to scream and holler and let him know they were right there.

Karen and Darius were seated in the VIP section surrounded by what she could only assume was his entourage. He told her that these were the guys who typically hung out with him all the time. Some of them were actually on his payroll as bodyguards. But since he'd been home, he'd been using them less. She didn't know if that was wise. But she didn't say anything. The club scene certainly wasn't what she'd had in mind when she told him he could take her anywhere he wanted. She'd been thinking of his place—more specifically, his bedroom.

She'd gone home and changed from her usual uniform of crinkled skirt, T-shirt and Isis-style Birkenstocks. She'd had a feeling her red skirt and her red, white and blue "Peace Is Patriotic" T-shirt weren't dressy enough for the nightclub Darius said he wanted to take her to. So she went home, took a quick shower, oiled up the skin with some shea butter, did the minimalist makeup thing she only did on special occasions and put on the red, black and green minidress she had gotten from Amina's attic.

She'd had the dress dry-cleaned weeks ago and was saving it for a special occasion. Since she didn't want to ruin the look of the dress, she wore a pair of strappy sandals instead of her normal Birkenstocks or Converse sneakers. No matter what Amina said, Karen did own some things that weren't "crunchy granola." And judging by the way Darius looked at her when he came to pick her up, changing into the minidress and strappy sandals had been a good idea.

She had to admit that watching him in his element with his boys in the club having fun was a little intriguing. He was very much the center of attention, the man in control, the one everyone looked to, the alpha male. And oddly enough, against everything she ever would have imagined about herself, she found that extremely attractive.

She found herself just gazing at him, hardly hearing what he was saying but totally enraptured by the shape of his mouth and the curve of his lips. She remembered what it felt like to kiss him, and automatically her nipples started to pebble and a warm energy flowed across her chest and into her heart. She hoped that she would be able to kiss him again by the end of the night.

She did a double take because she thought she saw the black and white Bobbsey twins from the other night at the Italian restaurant in the VIP room of the club. But when she looked again, they weren't there. She felt hyperaware and was starting to feel just a little bit out of place.

"You wanna dance?" Darius stood up and held out his hand.

Ne-Yo and Jamie Foxx's "She Got Her Own" was playing. Darius wrapped his arms around her and pulled her super close. They swayed back and forth to the groove, and she started to smell that unique scent again that she had come to only associate with him. She didn't think it was his cologne, because she knew she'd never smelled anything like it before.

She pressed her face to his muscular chest, inhaled deeply and felt an almost drugging effect. Who knew that nutmeg, summer rain and desire could have such an impact it damn near made a person woozy? At least it made her woozy. She inhaled again before tilting her head, gazing up at him.

He stared at her for a moment and then bent his head and captured her lips in a kiss. The slight brush of his mouth on hers gave way to an intensity that took her breath away. Their lips opened simultaneously, and their tongues seemed to play a sensuous game of hide-and-go-seek. Her tongue darted out to chase his before rushing back into her own mouth to savor the traces of him left there. His tongue came out searching for hers in order to tag her in a game so sublime she knew one of them had to stop or they would lose sense of the fact that they were in the middle of a dance floor in the small club.

She pulled away and immediately regretted it. The sense of loss was that instant, that deep.

His hand continued to caress her back, and he continued to hold her in his arms. It felt like he had held her like that forever, and she didn't ever want him to stop.

Where in the world were all these feelings coming from? Luckily, a faster club classic started playing, a fast dance track that was mostly instrumental with a pounding beat. She stepped out of his arms and started to move to the music, shaking her hips and moving her feet with every ounce of seduction inside of her.

"I see somebody has moves," Darius said with a smile as he put his hands back on her waist and started to dance to the faster beat. "I don't care if the music is fast or slow. I need to touch you." He winked playfully, but his request was made in a tone so serious it almost felt like a demand.

She wanted to tell him that he could have been touching her all he wanted if they had gone back to her place or his instead of coming to the club, but she didn't. She just grinned at her wicked thoughts and winked back at him.

He took a deep breath and inhaled. "What's that perfume you're wearing? Your scent has been driving me crazy. It's subtle most of the time, and then it kicks up and makes me want you in the worst way, like the air becomes charged with you. Whatever that is, I'm buying you boxes and boxes of the stuff so that you can wear it all the time."

She frowned. "I'm not wearing any perfume. A lot of people are allergic to scents. So, I try to be sensitive and not wear anything but some good old shea butter."

"Stop playing, girl. It smells like honey and hibiscus and dew and—" He stopped and frowned for a moment before shaking his head and laughing. "Well, it must be your natural sweet scent then." He bent his head and inhaled.

She chuckled nervously and thought that it would have been a great time to ask him what else he was wearing besides Cool Water cologne. She knew the cologne wasn't the scent she smelled when the attraction heated up between them.

She'd read articles in the occasional women's magazine about attraction, subconscious scents and pheromones. But what they seemed to be experiencing kicked all of that stuff—which she used to think was total crap, by the way—up about ten thousand notches.

"You have an interesting scent yourself, Mr. Rollins."

Go for broke, girl. You can do it. Either he'll think you're crazy or he'll be able to confirm what you're feeling.

She sighed. "It's almost like the air is constantly charged with desire when you're around me. It's subtle for the most part, but then out of the blue it feels like the air becomes superfilled with you and only you. And it makes me want to be with you in the worst way. It's not reasonable or rational, and it doesn't make any sense at all. Because I just met you, and I shouldn't want you this much."

He stopped dancing and stared at her, taking deep, staggered breaths. His hooded gaze roamed her body and made her hotter and hotter. She became so overheated that in the far-back regions of her mind she worried she might just forget her views about public displays of affection and start making out on the dance floor again.

"We should go." He took her hand and led her off the dance floor.

They said goodbye to all of his friends, and they were out of the club and into his car fairly quickly.

"I hope you don't mind coming to my place tonight?" He turned to her before starting the car.

"No. I don't mind at all."

They rode in silence, and she wasn't sure how she felt about that. There was so much she wanted to say. There was so much she wasn't sure *how* to say.

His loft apartment was stunning. She couldn't believe he had all this space in the city and rarely used it. Her tiny apartment times five could probably fit in his loft easily with room for five more and probably five more after that! The building had an around-the-clock door person, and there were only ten other tenants, two luxury lofts on each floor.

A professional must have decorated Darius's loft, Karen thought as she looked around. She couldn't help but think she was in a high-end showroom. There wasn't a lot of furniture, but what was there made a statement.

"Have a seat, and I'll open a bottle of wine."

She sat down on the cappuccino leather sectional, admiring the clean lines of the piece. There was also a matching cappuccino leather ottoman that doubled as a sofa table and two very modern-styled chairs in the space allotted for the living room. The living room was centered in such a way that she could see all other areas of the loft except for the walled-off master suite and the bathrooms. The chrome dining table in the dining area echoed the two chrome end tables in the living room. All she could think as she took in all of the furniture and expensive art was that someone had certainly paid a lot of attention to every detail.

He came over and handed her a glass of wine before sitting down right next to her. She took a sip and decided that she should put all her cards on the table and tell him about the journal, Dicey's reading, the dreams, all of it. If he thought she was crazy and kicked her to the curb—and she wasn't so sure anymore that she wasn't certifiable—then at least it would happen before he kissed her again and made her yearn for more.

So she spilled and told him everything that had happened since she picked up the journal in Amina's attic. And he listened, taking an occasional sip of wine but all the while listening intently.

When she finally finished, she took a deep breath and then took a gulp of her own wine. "Crazy, right?"

He took her glass from her and got up, taking the wineglasses back to the kitchen. When he returned, he sat on the ottoman right in front of her. He took her hands in his.

"Let me ask you this. If you weren't having all of this woo-woo stuff—as you call it—going on, do you think you would still be attracted to me? Would a brother still have a chance to kick it to you?"

"Do you mean if I was just minding my own business and the famous rapper and actor D-Roc came up to me would I talk to him?" She gave him a look that answered her own question. *Are you kidding me? Of course.*

"Even without all that fame and stuff…just me, the man, Darius Rollins. Would he have a chance with you if he wasn't D-Roc and you weren't having these dreams, just strip all of that away and then what?" He squeezed her hands before continuing, and her heart started pounding loudly in her chest.

"Because I have been having dreams, too, and I feel like I've known you forever even though I only met you a few days ago. And I feel compelled to just stop all this talking, take you to bed and make love to you until you can't think of anything else but me for the rest of your life. But when I strip all of that away and really think about you the woman, and if I would still want to be with you if all of that wasn't bouncing around in the background, I would have to say yes. I'm so impressed with you, the work you're doing in the neighborhood, your wit, your passion, your fire. The way you look in that dress. I would want you even if my soul wasn't demanding that I claim you right now."

"Right now?"

"Right now!" He leaned forward, and his lips lightly feathered hers, pulling away too soon. "But I need to know where you're coming from because for me none of that other stuff matters. Call it ego, call it caveman antics, call it arrogance, call it what you want. I need to know that you're here right now because you want to be here and you want to be here with me. All that other stuff will either work itself out or it won't. But I know that once I make love to you there won't be any turning back for either of us."

Dang it if the strength and determination in his voice wasn't making her nipples tighten and pebble to an almost painful point. She wanted—no, she needed—to make love to him more than she had ever wanted anyone before.

But she tried to push all of that to the back of her mind and focus on and answer his question.

She thought about Darius the man. He was a man who believed in hard work and achieved success in two cutthroat fields where the path to success was anything but easy. He was a man who cared about his family enough to want to continue to take care of them financially. He was a man who felt guilty enough about his cousin's death that he would volunteer in order to touch the lives of other youths so that they wouldn't end up losing their lives. He was handsome, sturdy, steady and strong. He made her smile and made her laugh, and he was *hella* fine. He was the kind of guy any girl would want to have a relationship with. Of course, she would want him in her life if he wasn't a superstar, if he was just hardworking Darius from the hood.

She nodded. "If this weird woo-woo stuff wasn't going on and you weren't a superstar, I'd still want to know you, Darius. I'd still want to be with you."

He smiled. "Good. Then let's try and focus on each other, on getting to know each other and building a relationship. And if the dreams continue and if you still smell like honey, hibiscus, dew and desire, it's all good. Even if we were somehow together in our past lives, it doesn't matter now. All that matters now is what we have in the present, what we build now."

"That makes sense. I guess… But what if we were supposed to learn something from the past, if it is all supposed to mean something…more?"

"Then we'll figure it out. But right now…right now I need you more than I need air." He stood and lifted her from the sofa so quickly that she thought he might drop her.

She wrapped her arms around his neck and held on. At the end of the day, she wanted what was about to happen more than she wanted anything else at the moment.

Chapter 12

Darius didn't have any second thoughts or hesitation about taking the next step with Karen. The sincerity in her eyes when she said she would want to know him and be with him whether he was a superstar or not or despite the unexplainable attraction they felt for one another made him feel ten feet tall.

More than he needed to make this woman his, he needed her to fully and completely *want* to be his. He refused to accept anything less.

When they entered his bedroom, he stood her on her own two feet and stood in front of her, taking her in for the umpteenth time that evening. The red minidress with the black-and-green pattern was so her. And she seemed so familiar to him in that moment, like he'd seen her in that exact dress countless times and it always had the power to slay him. The material hugged her curves perfectly. Her long, brown legs glistened and beckoned for him to reach out and stroke them.

"Take off your dress." He spoke the words in a barely controlled rumble. He wanted to see more. He wanted to see all of her.

She slid the dress over her head and tossed it to the side. Standing there in black lace matching bra and panties, along with those strappy high-heeled sandals, she looked like she was ready for a Victoria's Secret photo shoot.

He could see more of her than he had ever seen, and still it wasn't enough.

"Take off your bra. Slowly."

She reached behind her back and unsnapped the bra before slowly removing one strap at a time and letting them fall off her shoulders to create the perfect picture of spillage before taking it all the way off and casting it to the side.

His pulse quickened, and his mind raced. He could swear he already knew that the sex between them was going to be both familiar and unlike anything they had ever experienced. He couldn't wait, because he knew it would be like coming home and also like finding a place of joy, happiness and completion that you never in your wildest dreams thought could exist.

"Lie down on the bed."

She did exactly what he told her to do, and the man inside of him bursting at the seams to possess this woman seemed to be beating on his chest with each act.

He got on the bed and took off her sandals, one at a time, caressing her feet as he did. He then slid off her thong. Better he get the thing out of the way intact now than rip it off and ruin it later.

He touched her and found her wet and ready. He used two of his fingers and stroked her steadily. She squirmed, letting out a soft sigh when he added a third finger. He removed his fingers, and she groaned until he kissed her, kissing away any complaints. His mouth covered hers, and he feasted on her lips and tongue and mouth as if her saliva had life-saving properties.

His hands roamed her soft, sensuous body for a long time as he kissed her. He let his fingers explore her sex again, and this time he delved into her wet, heated folds and touched her until he felt her shaking and heard the muffled cries of her release. He felt her inner walls gripping his fingers and let them squeeze and squeeze until her body went limp.

He pulled away from the kiss and just looked at her. She was amazing.

She let out a breath. "Hey, this is no fair. You still have your clothes on. Don't I get to touch you, too?" She reached her hands under his shirt and made an attempt to lift it.

"In time, in time." He slid down her body and gave her the most intimate of kisses, starting with her navel and working his way down to her slick, heated womanhood.

Her recent orgasm had left plenty of her nectar to feast on, but he wanted more. So he licked, nipped and thrust his tongue in and out, around and around, back and forth and as deep as it could go. His face almost seemed to merge with her sex as his nose tickled her clitoris and his cheeks brushed her thighs.

When he felt her legs begin to shake, he held them tightly, making sure she couldn't escape and take all her sweet nectar away. Her soft, panting breaths and pleas to please make love to her now only made him want to taste her more. He lost all sense of time, and it was only the sharp cry of release and almost-violent shuddering of her last orgasm that pulled him out of his zone.

He stood and began to take off his clothes, all the while admiring how sexy she looked in the throes of passion. Her soft, honey-complexioned skin shimmered with slight perspiration, and her auburn and bronze locs were fanned out on the rust comforter. She looked like an alluring sun goddess. Her eyes were closed and a very satisfied half smile tilted her lips. As he placed the protection on and joined her on the bed, he hoped she was ready for some more.

Karen felt the bed shift and opened her eyes in spite of the fact that she was more than happy to just lounge there basking in the aftermath. But then she saw him…this perfect bronzed sculpted figure of masculine perfection inching onto the bed and onto her body. The ripples on his chest made her want to reach out and touch. So she did.

She lifted her hand and let it glide softly up and down, marveling in his form and knowing that the real thing was so much better than all those pictures of him shirtless on his album covers and on magazine covers. She had to remix Marvin Gaye because Darius's chest made her wanna holler and touch with both her hands. So she did. She stroked her hands up and down his chest, anticipating how it would feel when he was right up on her, body to body, his hard steel pressed against her soft curves.

It would feel so good.

She looked up at his face as she continued to explore his chest. His hooded gaze foretold of a barely contained passion ready to be unleashed. She could tell that he was holding everything in, trying to give her time to explore him since he had explored her so thoroughly and completely. Her eyes traveled down from his face, stopping momentarily to admire his pecs again but moving on to find him poised, wrapped in protection and ready for the taking.

And she planned to take it all. Over and over again.

She spread her legs and pulled him down to her, capturing his lips. Her tongue traced his lips before diving into his mouth, tasting herself there.

She moaned as she mused that nothing should feel this good. Nothing should feel this right.

He let her control the kiss for a moment before taking over. His strong lips took the lead, and she was glad to let him.

He took her bottom lip between his teeth and nipped, sending a sweet jolt up her spine. Staring at her intently, he licked the spot and pulled away.

His hands trailed her body before stopping on her hips. His hands curved around her backside, and he gently lifted her hips off the bed, lining her at the perfect angle for his first thrust.

She could hear her own heartbeat as she waited.

He placed one of her legs over his shoulder, the other on his hip and slowly leaned into her.

The first teasing contact made her breath catch.

Tingles assaulted her body instantly. He penetrated her slowly, surely and masterfully, taking his time and delving inch by magnificent inch until she was fuller than she had ever been. Her sex hugged his with no room to spare. She closed her eyes and tried to get used to the breadth and depth of him. He held himself, giving her ample time to get used to his size. And she moved her hips in desperation.

Perfection. That's what it felt like to be with him in that moment. Each stroke filled her until there was no room. Each withdrawal left her feeling almost bereft, the void was so profound. She needed him inside of her, pushing her further and further past her limits.

He pulled out until only the tip of his manhood was in her and thrust back in, repeating the action with such a frenzy and intensity she didn't know where he stopped and where she began. She tightened her legs around him, trying to hold him, trying to make it last forever.

"Forever." She didn't know what made her say that word. She just knew she had to say it.

His thrusts quickened. "Forever."

She moved her hips to meet each of his thrusts with measured movement. She bounced up and swayed, offering a swivel of her hips that allowed him to touch places inside of her that she never could have imagined. He clutched her hips, holding her still, and buried himself deeper with each thrust.

He pulled all the way out and penetrated again with a speed and precision so overwhelming that it left her breathless. She could feel the tingles overtaking her from the inside out, from her core to the tiny hair follicles on her skin and back again. It wasn't long before her body was shaking and her head shook back and forth on its own accord. She could feel her locs wiping across her face. She closed her eyes tight as she felt the strongest orgasm she had ever felt rip through her.

"Darius!" She screamed out his name, and she didn't know why. "Darius," she called out to him again, softer this time but no less needful.

She reached out to him, and he bent forward, kissing her deeply, sweetly but all the while moving his hips as if he were possessed.

Just when she thought she couldn't take any more, he whispered her name across her lips. He lifted her hips up all the way until they rested on his thighs and pulled her body up until they were torso to torso, connected, hard steel to soft curves. He held her tightly and said her name one more time before his own release caused him to grip her hips tighter and hold her closer to him.

They sat like that for minutes afterward, speechless, arms wound around each other. They were so close that their heartbeats and breathing seemed to be synchronized.

He gently laid her back down on the bed as he withdrew. She immediately missed the feel of him in her and around her. He went to dispose of the protection and came right back to bed, wrapping her in his arms again.

She sighed. Being held was exactly what she needed.

He kissed her forehead.

"That was the most amazing thing I have ever experienced. It's never been like that before. Ever." She didn't want to hold back any of what she was feeling, even though the last thing she wanted to do was come across as a sprung chicken-head.

"I know. It's never been like that for me either. Now do you see what I meant when I told you that us hooking up wasn't going to make what we were feeling go away or be any less intense? I knew it would be like this. I knew once I had you I wasn't going to be able to let you go…that I was going to want to hold on to you forever."

"Forever… Those are the words—"

"Shh." He placed his finger over her lips. "I know. But we said we weren't going to dwell in the past or, in our case, the past lives. I just want this connection to be about you and me. Darius and Karen. Here and now."

She nodded. "Okay. So what next?"

"What do you mean?"

"I mean. What next? What do we do next?"

"We continue to get to know each other. I continue to help out at the center until I have to go shoot my next movie. And when I do go and shoot my next movie, you're going to be the queen of the frequent-flyers club and I'll be the king because we're going to continue to see each other. And that's the gist of it. Sound good to you?"

"Sounds good to me." She sat up. "I guess I should be heading back to my place."

"Oh, no, baby. You're staying here with me tonight— and hopefully many more nights to come."

"But I have to work in the morning. And so do you, Mr. Volunteer of the Year."

"I know. We'll get up early, shower together and then

I'll swing you by your place and wait for you while you change clothes. Then we'll both drive in together."

"Hmm. Don't you have it all figured out, Mr. Rollins?"

"Yep."

"Okay, then. I guess that'll work." She wrapped her arms around her knees as she took in her surroundings for the first time. She'd barely gotten a chance to register what the room looked like when they'd first entered. She was too busy feeling everything that he had to offer her.

The bedroom looked like something out of a designer magazine. The bed was a huge king-size four-poster platform bed. The wood on all the furniture was stained a deep, dark chocolate-brown. The comforter was a beautiful rust shade and felt like silk against the skin. In fact, the more she looked at it the more she realized that it probably was raw silk.

She looked in the corner and saw an object that seemed so out of place that she couldn't help but ask him about it.

"What's up with that guitar? You turning into a rock star now?"

He held his head down for a minute as if the last thing he wanted to talk about was the guitar. Finally he looked her in the eye. "I've been teaching myself how to play, and I took a few lessons. I want my next album to be a little more musical."

"So you know how to play that thing? No way."

He got up, got the guitar and then sat back near her on the bed. "I've actually been working on a new song since I met you. It's a song about you and the work you're doing in the neighborhood."

She felt the heat rise from her neck to her cheeks.

He started strumming the chords. And soon a melody began to take shape. She could have sworn she'd heard the melody before.

"The melody is from Earth, Wind and Fire's 'Devotion.'" He played a little more of the melody and then he stopped and rapped the lyrics, alternating every so often with a human beat box that made her want to dance or at least sway with it.

She gives without
Thinking 'bout it
Don't talk about it
She be about it
The proof is in her deeds
And she don't have to shout about it.
Lifting as she climbs
Working for the people
All she needs is a man who's willin'
to meet her as her equal
I'm down for the task
Down for love that lasts
Forever is in her eyes
She's my future and my past
The reason why I rise
To be the best I can be
It's real, not a test
And her vibe is pressing me
To keep forward motion
To honor love, hope and emotion
To do what I can so I can match her devotion.

Then he started strumming the melody again and sang the hook from the Earth, Wind and Fire song.

She felt a tear run down her cheek. No one had ever done anything like that for her before.

"That was beautiful."

He blushed as he stopped playing the guitar. "I'm still working on the song. But I definitely want it to be on my next album." He put the guitar down and sat next to her.

"It's a little different from your usual songs. Do you think your fans will like the new direction?"

"Do you like the new direction?"

"I love it. How could I not? No one has ever tried to woo me by writing me a song before."

"Well, then, that's all that matters. You're all that matters." He kissed her, and for a minute she believed him.

Chapter 13

The next morning, Darius took Karen to her place to get dressed like they'd planned, and he had to smile at the T-shirt she was wearing. The purple T-shirt had a baby boy and a baby girl on it, and each was looking down into their own diapers. The caption read, "So that explains the difference in our pay?" She wore a pair of jeans that looked like they were made for her and poured onto her curves and some really cute purple Converse sneakers.

Her style was unlike any woman he had ever dated before, and he liked it. He found himself wondering what kind of T-shirt she was going to have on next. And he'd never look at a crinkle skirt the same way again. From now on, in his mind, crinkle skirts were the equivalent to sexy lingerie.

As they walked up to the center together, he noticed a guy standing in front of the center as if he were waiting for something. The guy was tall with black locs hanging down past his shoulders. He wore a white kufi hat, dashiki and matching pants. Small gold wire-framed glasses sat perched on his long nose. He didn't look particularly dangerous, but one couldn't be too careful these days.

Darius reached over to pull Karen close just in case the guy was a threat or something like that. But before he could she took off running and leaped into the man's arms. The man lifted her up and spun her around as she squealed with glee.

It was really hard not to become totally alpha male at that point and growl at the man who had the audacity to step into his territory and touch his woman. So, Darius decided he wasn't even going to try. That man had about two seconds to put Karen down or all hell was going to break loose.

After a second spin, the man put her down, but he still had his arm wrapped around her. "Queen, it is so good to see you. You're looking stunning as ever." The man had a slight accent that Darius couldn't quite place, and he also couldn't tell if it was real or fake.

"Saul! I can't believe you're back. When did you get back from the motherland? And please tell me you'll be back at the center. The kids have missed you around here." Karen had a smile on her face that would have chased any bad feelings Darius was having away if it were just the two of them and this interloper didn't still have his arm around her.

Darius cleared his throat, and the two of them looked up.

"Oh, where are my manners, I was so excited to see

Saul that I didn't even introduce the two of you. Saul, this is Darius. You might know him as the rapper and actor D-Roc. He grew up in the East New York neighborhood, and he's donating some of his time between movies to help out at the center."

Darius bit back a frown at her introduction. He was more than a volunteer at the center, more than a rapper or actor. He was her man, and Saul needed to take his arms off of her, pronto.

Saul reached out with the arm that wasn't around Karen and offered it for a handshake. Darius shook his hand somewhat begrudgingly.

"And Darius, this is Saul. He's an old friend from college. And he has been with the center from the beginning—our first volunteer, our first employee. He's an activist, a poet and all-around cool guy. For the past six months, he's been on the continent of Africa taking in the motherland. And I can't wait to hear all about it!"

Darius and Saul looked each other in the eyes as Karen spoke, and Darius could have sworn he saw a hint of an unspoken threat there, as if Saul was staking or restaking some kind of claim on Karen. Darius narrowed his eyes and shook his head.

"It's nice to meet you, man. Welcome back to the States. What countries in Africa did you visit? I've been to parts of Ghana, South Africa, Swaziland, Kenya and Egypt to perform." Darius reached over and pulled Karen into his arms. "I'll have to take you with me next time, Karen. You would really love it." He squeezed her and gave her a peck on the lips that intensified slightly before she seemed to realize that they weren't alone.

She touched his cheek and turned to Saul. "So are you back for a while? Or are you back at least long enough to tell me all about your trip?"

"My Queen, I'm back for a while, and hopefully, my old job is still here for me. Or I can volunteer until we get the grants to pay me. You know how we do it." Saul reached out and caressed Karen's cheek.

Oh, hell, no! A low growl came out of Darius's mouth, and Saul stepped back.

"Sorry, brother, I mean no disrespect. It's just the Queen and I go way back, and she'll always have a special place in my heart." Saul gave a little bow and stepped back.

"It's all good. Just try and respect the fact that she and I are building something now and whatever y'all had in the past needs to stay in the past." Darius felt his chest puffing up with each word. He didn't want to start out his morning strapping with some chump in African garb. But he would if he had to. Even though he never in a million years would have thought that he'd be fighting over a woman, period, he knew he'd take on the world for Karen.

Karen gave a nervous chuckle. "Okay, calm down, Rocky. We're all peace here. Saul and I aren't like that, so there's no need to get all territorial." She gave both he and Saul a pointed look.

"You don't have to worry about me. I'm here for the youth. I'd never do anything to jeopardize the work." Saul jokingly put his hands up as if to say he was innocent.

Darius knew the man was anything but innocent. And he also knew that if he gave Saul any opening whatsoever he'd be back in there trying to get with Karen. That wasn't going to happen.

"You don't have to worry about me, Karen." *As long as Saul respects my place and stays in his damn lane, everything will be fine with me!*

"Good. Remember, we are setting examples for the youth. Speaking of which, we need to get the center opened for the start of the new day." Karen took her keys out and went toward the gate before stopping and looking next door.

"That's odd. Dicey's sign is gone, and her place looks empty." She walked over and looked through the metal bars of the gate into the storefront. "It is empty in there! And with all those huge dust bunnies, it looks like it's been empty for a while. But I was just in there yesterday. That's odd." Karen turned to Darius. "You remember seeing the sign that said 'Divine Intuition,' right? Did the tall, beautiful chocolate sister with long goddess braids ever ask you if she could give you a reading?"

Darius's mind was still on Saul, and he really couldn't remember what had been beside the center or even if there had been a store next door at all. Since he'd set eyes on Karen, he really couldn't think about much else but her. He peeped through the window. "I really can't recall what was next door. But if anyone was, they sure got out of there quick, fast and in a hurry."

Karen frowned. "She'd been there for about a year. Saul, do you remember meeting her? Do you remember the palm-reading shop that was next door?"

Saul shook his head. "Sorry, Queen, all I remember is you...and the youth, of course. But I'll try and recall this Dicey person as soon as we get inside and open up.

It's good to be back!" He looked like he was going to try and pick Karen up and spin her around again. But he glanced at Darius and stepped back instead.

Darius narrowed his eyes and reached for Karen's keys. "I'll get this gate up."

He opened up the center and they went inside, but he couldn't help but wonder how much trouble this Saul person was going to be.

Karen walked into the youth center more than a little perplexed. She couldn't figure out why just yesterday she had gone into Dicey's place for a reading and today it looked like no one had been there in years. Given everything that had been happening in her life the past few weeks since she found that journal, she shouldn't have been too surprised. But this was too woo-woo even for the turn her life had taken. If she didn't know better, she would start to question her sanity. Maybe that's what this was all about. Maybe her life was turning into one cosmic psychic woo-woo practical joke.

Once they opened up, Darius offered to do a morning discussion session about achieving goals with youth who were interested. And of course almost all of them were interested. She loved the center in the summer when the kids were out of school and things were really bustling.

She was so busy thinking about the disappearance of the Divine Ms. Dicey that she almost forgot about the testosterone battle that had been waged in front of the center that morning.

What in the world had gotten into those two? She had half a mind to tell them both to take a long hike off a short cliff.

Darius didn't have anything to worry about as far as she and Saul were concerned. Sure, they went back a long way, all the way back to their college days at Brooklyn College. And, yes, they had been comrades, marched against just about every social injustice known to man and sat in too many sit-ins and building takeovers to count, but they hadn't been together in years. They had been FWB in the past whenever they weren't dating other people. But they'd both agreed that they were way too similar to ever make a play for a relationship.

After she finished making sure that everything was running smoothly and folks were where they were supposed to be, she went back into her office with Saul.

"So, Queen, what's up with you and the rapper? He seems a little territorial, don't you think?" Saul leaned back in his chair looking rather suave and a little too pleased with himself. The white cotton dashiki and kufi hat made his deep-chocolate skin look all the more striking.

Handsome devil!

"You got jokes? I thought I was going to have to pull the two of you apart. What was that about? You know it's not even like that between us."

"Oh, Queen, you slay my heart! How can you say that? How can you deny that what we have is special? We always come back together."

"Um, we were never really *together,* Saul. So don't even try it. We both knew we would never work as a couple. We've always said that. Don't go trying to flip the script now."

"What? A man can't change his mind? Maybe I

realized some things when I was in the motherland. Maybe I realized my true African Queen was in Brooklyn after all?" Saul smiled, showing all of his perfectly straight pearly whites.

She remembered that before he left they had joked that he was going off to finally find his African Queen and would probably come back married or engaged if he came back at all. Saul had always been one of those brothers who loved everything African. While they had both minored in black studies at Brooklyn College, Saul was the one doing all the suggested outside readings, taking more than the required classes and going to every lecture that had something to do with the continent.

She even teased him all the time about the slight accent he had picked up through hanging around with brothers and sisters from the Caribbean and from various countries in Africa. People who just met him always tried to place his accent. And Karen always chuckled to herself, because she knew the man was from Bedford-Stuyvesant, also known as Bed-Stuy. And as far as she knew, his family migrated north from Alabama, not the motherland or one of the islands.

"Anyway…as you can see, your *Queen* is more than a little busy right now. I don't want to jinx it. But I think I've found *the one,* the honest-to-goodness pick-up-the-phone-call-mama-and-tell-her-all-about-him one! So, don't you start no mess." She pointed her finger at him in mock warning.

He clutched his heart and frowned. "You can't be serious. He's the exact opposite of everything you believe in. I'd be surprised if he had a political bone in his body. You must be kidding me. Tell me it's a lie."

"I can't tell you that, because it's true. Now shut up and be happy for me. And wish me luck. I really like Darius a lot." She knew she was way beyond like when it came to Darius. But she didn't think Saul had to know that now.

"Fine. Fine. You've become a little testy in the past six months, haven't you? Anyway, fill me in on what's been going on here. We can talk about my trip to Africa over dinner. How about some Ethiopian food? My treat? We'll eat…catch up…"

"I would love to have dinner on your dime, but I'll have to check with Darius. He might have plans."

"Oh, now see. That's just wrong. An old friend has to stand in line for dinner these days? What is the world coming to?"

"Dinner?" Darius would pick that moment to walk into her office. His eyebrow was slightly arched, and he folded his arms across his chest.

Saul stood up, and she feared the testosterone battle was about to start a round two. She got up from her desk and walked over to Darius.

"Yes, Saul invited me out to have Ethiopian food while he tells me all about his trip. But I told him that I had to check to see if you had any plans for us this evening." She placed her arm around him.

She could tell that his teeth had been clenched for a minute, and slowly his face loosened and gave way to a practiced smile.

"In fact, I do have plans for us this evening. You and I have a date. And it's a surprise, so don't even ask." Darius leaned over and pecked her on the lips quickly. "I just wanted to let you know after this second group of students that I'm going to head over to the studio and lay down a track or two. But I'll be back for you by six so that we can start our date."

Darius gave Saul a pointed look. "It was nice meeting you, brother. I guess I'll see you around. And who knows, maybe Karen and I both will be able to go out for Ethiopian food with you and hear all about your trip." The expression on his face clearly said, *Not!*

"Yeah, nice meeting you, too, brother. It's not every day I get to meet a big superstar. Wish I could say I liked your work, but I'm into music with a message and I've never bought into that Hollywood crap. But hey, everybody has a different calling." Saul shrugged.

Karen cringed because Saul's self-righteous rant reminded her of how she must have sounded a couple of days ago when she went on and on about only listening to political hip-hop and Darius's goody-two-shoes image. She couldn't believe she'd been such a jerk and how dramatically her feelings about him had shifted.

My, how quickly things change....

Darius looked at her as if he knew exactly what she was thinking and winked. "Yeah, you probably like a lot of the same music as my baby here. Good thing she didn't let her taste in music stop her from giving me a chance." He winked again and gave her another, longer kiss.

She wrapped her arms around his neck and pulled him closer. She probed his mouth as if she were looking for all the lost treasures in the world. And judging by the tingles that traveled up and down her arms, she was finding them. He wrapped his arms around her and pulled her even closer. His hands clasped her bottom, and more tingles shot through her. Before she knew it, she let out a deep moan and everything intensified.

"All right, all right! Point taken, brother. Point taken. I get it." Saul's voice interrupted their embrace. "And you two need to go get a room. You never used to like public displays of affection."

Karen could feel the heat rising, and she knew her cheeks were probably redder than red. How did she forget that Saul was in the room? What was Darius doing to her? She turned and saw that Saul was giving them a glaring look.

Darius pulled away but not before giving her a pat on the behind. "I'll try and stop back in before I leave for the studio. But if you're still catching up with Saul, just know that I'll be back for you at six." Darius left the room, and all the air seemed to come back.

"Man, you have it bad. I've never seen you this gaga over a guy. You certainly were never this gaga over me. I guess he just might be the one."

Karen touched her kiss-swollen lips and walked back over to her desk. "Anyway, that's pretty much the most exciting thing that's happened in my life since you've been gone. Amina finally moved to South Carolina like she's been threatening to do for years. I've been scrambling like crazy to get some more grants so that we can make some improvements and possibly hire some more folks so that we can help more kids around here. You know how hectic things get in the summer. We have more need than we could possibly fill on our current budget. *And* I think I just met my soul mate."

"Soul mate? Isn't that pushing it a little? I mean, come on…the two of you have nothing in common. I have more in common with you than he does." Saul let out an irritated hiss. "Look, whatever, if he's your soul mate then I'm happy for you. If he isn't, I'll be here when he's gone, just like I always am. I just hope he doesn't play you or anything. What do you really know about this guy?" Saul gave her a pointed look.

"But whatever...listen, I have your back on those grants. You know I'm your go-to guy for getting funding. I haven't met a grant yet that I can't get. Point me in the direction of those applications, Queen."

She smiled. Saul was always able to bring more money into the center. She was so glad that he was back. Things were working out perfectly.

"I'm going to go check up on things in the center. The most recent grant applications are in the top file cabinet. Have a look. And take your pick of the vacant offices. It's good to have you back. We have funding to pay you for a part-time position, and hopefully, we'll get one of those grants and be able to pay you full-time." She gave him a hug. "It's great to have you back, Saul. I missed you."

"Me, too, Queen. Me, too."

Chapter 14

After speaking to the second group of kids at the center, Darius went over to the studio and started laying down the track for the song he wrote for Karen. His label mate, the heartthrob R & B singer Deuce Songz, just happened to be in the studio next to the one Darius was in. And luckily, he was able to sing the hook.

Darius knew he could carry a tune, and he probably could have sung the hook himself, but he wanted the song to be perfect. He still couldn't believe that he was in the studio recording a song for a woman, but he'd never met a woman like Karen before.

As they played the song back, he knew it was going to be a smash. Rappers had been rapping love ballads ever since LL Cool J dropped "I Need Love," but this song was about his love for her, her love for the people and how she made him want to be a better man. It was the ultimate love song. He could just hear the radio announcers introducing the hot new hit from D-Roc and Deuce Songz.

Every head was nodding in the studio, and Darius loved that. The only person who wasn't feeling the vibe was Cullen.

"That was a waste of studio time. What the hell was that? Your fans want another party anthem from you, not this crap!" Cullen busted into a rampage as soon as the music ended.

Darius spun around and glared at Cullen. Darius waved his hands, dismissing everyone from the studio. The room cleared immediately.

Cullen didn't seem fazed by the suddenly empty room, but then no one ever accused the man of being a genius.

"What the hell is your problem, Cullen? You wanted me in the studio. I'm in the studio. I just cut a track that is going to have all my female fans wishing I was talking about them, and it might even get me some new fans from the backpack group. Everyone in here was feeling the song. But even more than that, *I* feel the song."

"That song is wack. And your female fans won't support it, because what they want to hold on to is the fantasy that they can have you. You rapping this lovey-dovey crap won't make them happy. And I noticed you didn't mention your men fans. Because you know the few you do have, the few who don't already think you're not hard-core will think you've completely gone soft after they hear this crap."

Cullen ran his hand across his head. "I blame that youth center bitch for this crap. She's to blame. It's like she's Erykah Badu, and you're Common. The next thing you know she'll have you rocking freakin' crochet pants with a matching hat." He sucked his teeth in disgust.

Darius grabbed Cullen by the throat and jacked him up against the wall. "I won't tell you again about calling her out of her name. Her name is Karen. If you can't remember that, then call her Ms. Williams. But you damn well better start showing some respect or I will gladly show you why people should never underestimate a guy just because they don't think he's hard-core. I won't tolerate you or anyone else disrespecting her." He let Cullen slide down from the wall. "Now get the hell out of here. If my label isn't feeling the song, then I'll take it into consideration. But I've got work to do, and you're ruining my vibe."

Cullen brushed off his suit jacket and glared at Darius. "You're lucky I realize you're just whipped right now and not thinking straight. That's the power of the pussy. Boy oh boy, it really makes men crazy. Be careful, boy, men have been killed for less disrespect than you've just shown. I'll leave and let you record. Hopefully, you have something better to offer than that crap you just put down."

Cullen strutted out of the studio, and Darius was almost tempted to go after the man and really jack him up. But he had more music to make and a beautiful woman to go see in a few hours. He didn't want anything standing in the way of him going to see Karen.

Cullen angrily pulled out his cell phone as he walked to his car. He dialed the number of the person who was going to help him take care of this Karen Williams problem once and for all.

"Are you back where I need you?" Cullen asked.

"I'm here, and I don't appreciate being summoned like this. I was chilling in Miami, having a good time with a lot of good-looking blondes when you so rudely interrupted me."

"Yeah, whatever, I need you to hurry up and handle this Karen problem. I need some hard proof in place quick to get her out of the picture before she derails my gravy train. And if you don't want it leaked who pulled the trigger on Shemar Sunyetta then you need to get your girl in check." Cullen put the threat out there even though the last thing he wanted was anyone looking into Shemar's murder. Because if they found the triggerman, it might not be too long before they found out who paid the triggerman.

"Yeah, we both know that you want that to stay buried as much as I do. Plus no one saw me shoot Shemar. There were no witnesses and no evidence." He let out an exasperated sigh.

Cullen didn't have the heart to tell the idiot that he had all the proof he needed about who shot Shemar. He'd paid someone to videotape the murder, and it was one of his favorite snuff films. He watched it often.

"Look, it really shouldn't take that long for me to break them up—although they are a lot closer than I would have imagined. She never seemed like the type to get that open over a brother."

"I don't want to hear all this," Cullen snapped. "I just need you to follow through. I'd hate for her to find out what happened to some of the grant money she got for the center. She probably won't like to know how much you skimmed off the top to finance that move to

Miami. I wonder if she knows that's what they're calling the *motherland* these days. And some of those grants were federal grants. Mmm…I'm sure you don't want that leaking out." Cullen made a threat he was more than willing to carry out if only for the way he knew that particular truth would break the little bitch.

He chuckled. Sometimes people were just entirely too trusting.

There was a long pause, and Cullen wondered if the line had gone dead. "Hello, cat got your tongue?"

"I said I'd get you what you needed, man. There's no need to keep on with these threats. Karen and D-Roc are about to be history before they even get a chance to begin. I have the papers you need me to get her to sign, and I'll have them to you by tonight. And trust me when I say this is the last thing you'll get from me. The next time, I'm going to disappear so deep that you'll never be able to find me. I'll stick around to make sure the deed is done and maybe hit that a couple more times after he dumps her ass…but I'm out of here after this, and you can just forget you know me!"

The next thing Cullen heard was the dial tone.

That was fine with him. He had a couple more phone calls to make to put things in place for good.

They wouldn't know what hit them by the time he was done with them.

Karen was finishing up her lecture notes for the big talk she planned to give at the "Planning for College Fair" she would be having at the center in a few weeks. She knew it was the middle of summer, but she liked to have her college fair before the fall started. She found that some disadvantaged families needed the extra time to really start planning and getting ready for making that transition. The applications and financial-aid forms alone were enough to turn a lot of people around and discourage them from trying. That's why she brought in folks from the local universities' financial aid and admissions offices to give how-to workshops all day at the fair and to offer help with those kinds of forms all year long. She found that the people who attended the fair in the summer were more successful at doing the things they needed to do to get their kids into college.

Since she tried to switch it up so that she wasn't saying the same thing every year, she was usually finishing up her speech right up until the very last minute. She stretched and stood up from her chair, moving her neck from side to side.

Saul came into her office with his usual perfect smile in place. "I have some documents for your signature. I even found a few grants online that you hadn't found yet. I told you I was the money getter." He placed a stack of papers in front of her. "The only thing is some of them have quick deadlines. A few have to be postmarked today. So, I'm gonna need you to sign them quickly so I can catch the post office, Queen."

"You are a godsend. I'm so glad you're back, Saul." She pulled out her pen and signed the grant applications. It was just like having her right-hand man back. She was glad that he'd gotten a chance to travel to the motherland and live out one of his dreams. But she really meant it when she said things hadn't been the same without him. "I'll see you tomorrow. I'll probably just lock up once

Darius gets here. Maybe we can grab lunch on Friday and you can tell me all about the motherland."

Saul took the papers up from the desk.

"Oh, yeah, wait a minute. You're gonna need some postage for those. Darius used all our postage the other day. Let me get some money out of the slush fund for you." She grabbed a twenty out of the lock box that held the petty cash she kept on-site for quick small purchases. "Be sure to bring back a receipt. We have to show where every penny goes around here."

"Sure thing, Queen. I'll see you." Saul walked out, and she went back to her speech.

"Now, I never would have guessed this in a million years." Karen walked hand in hand with Darius down the crowded boardwalk. "Coney Island? You just didn't strike me as a Coney Island kind of a guy."

They had ridden several of the rides, including the world-famous Cyclone, and now they were strolling on the boardwalk eating cotton candy and enjoying the lights. Darius had worn his New York Yankees fitted baseball cap low and a pair of shades. He looked like any other average brother, and no one seemed to recognize him at all. She still felt honored that he would risk being recognized and mobbed to give her an evening at Coney Island. It meant a lot.

"I figured this is something you probably wouldn't take the time to do yourself. And it is something I remember doing a few times when I was a kid, but I haven't done it in a while. My aunt Janice and I used to bring my little cousin Frankie here when he was a little kid, and truth be told, I think we used to have more fun than him."

"You're right, I probably wouldn't do something like this on my own. Things are always so hectic. We usually send a busload of kids from the center here at least once during the season. But I usually stay behind. Or if I go, I'm usually too busy making sure the kids and staff are all doing what they're supposed to do and not having much fun myself. So thank you. This is nice."

Darius polished off the last of his cotton candy and wrapped his arms around her. "Do you know what would be even nicer?"

"What?"

"A walk on the beach and a Nathan's hot dog."

She laughed and finished off her cotton candy. She would probably regret eating all the junk food later, but she wasn't going to think about it. "Okay, but I want extra onions and sauerkraut on mine."

He shook his head. "You're lucky I'd kiss you with onion breath or not. A little bit of onions won't stop me from devouring you later on tonight." He winked at her, and a shiver went down her spine.

She giggled. "Promises. Promises."

"Oh, you can take that to the bank, baby. I plan on tasting every inch of you tonight."

They purchased their hot dogs and walked along the beach. Karen had to admit that she'd never had such a fun and relaxing time. And even though she hadn't known him that long, Darius really was good for her. With him, she felt balanced for the first time in ages.

"One day, I'm going to take you to an exotic beach—

one that you can walk barefoot on. I wanna see those pretty toes sinking into the sand."

"This is absolutely perfect. I never realized how good it would feel to just relax for a minute. And I can't believe you have me this laid-back in such a short time. I would usually still be in my office applying for grants and trying to bring money into the center. It's a good thing Saul is back. He'll be able to pick up some of the slack now that I'm turning into this social butterfly."

She laughed, and she noticed that Darius was silent. "What's wrong?"

"Nothing. I just don't like Saul. I don't trust him."

"Okay, but do you trust me?" She really hoped that Darius didn't start that testosterone stuff tonight. If he ruined a perfectly nice evening and didn't follow through on his promise to kiss every inch of her body, then she was going to throw a fit. She really needed him to follow through on that promise! All of those intensely erotic dreams from the past, or their past lives, or whatever they were, had made her perpetually horny. She needed him again and again and again if possible.

"I trust you. It's just I can tell he wants you, and I swear that when he touched you I just about lost it this morning. I know you think I'm being an alpha jerk, but you're mine. And then he had the nerve to try and test me? Hinting around about what y'all might have had in the past. Somebody needs to tell dude…" He huffed and kicked the sand.

She sighed. "The past I had with Saul has nothing on the past I had with you. I know we said we weren't going to talk about it, but not talking about it isn't going to make the fact that we both had weird dreams and we both feel like we've known each other before go away. And then there is that freaky mess about Divine, Ms. Dicey or whatever her name was…telling me that you are my soul mate and then up and disappearing when I finally decide to give you a chance. My little FWB fling with Saul had nothing on our lifetimes of connections. Shoot. It has nothing on the way you made me feel in one night. So stop tripping."

She realized that he had stopped walking beside her, and she turned around. "What? What's wrong?"

His face wore an intense frown when he caught up to her. "First of all, too much damn information, Karen! Damn, you could have let a brother speculate and wonder about that shit. I didn't need to know that you and Saul were fuck buddies."

"Friends with benefits! And that was only a few times when we weren't with other people. What's the big deal? You knew I wasn't a virgin, right? I have had other lovers in this lifetime. Maybe you found me early in the past lives. But you were a little slow showing up this time, and a woman has needs." She chuckled and put her arms around his waist. "Oh, come on. That was funny. You know you want to laugh."

He shook his head. "You're lucky I can't stay mad at you." He laughed. "And you're lucky I know I put it on you so good that there ain't no way another man could ever compete."

"Modest, aren't you? Your humility is awe-inspiring!" *And you ain't neva lied,* she thought as she tilted her head sassily. She wasn't about to tell him how right he was when she could clearly see he didn't need any help in the ego department. She had to admit he talked like that because he could back it up!

"You know it's the truth, but you don't want to admit it because you think it might feed my ego. But just knowing that you know it is good enough for me."

She frowned. The man must be a mind reader. She rolled her eyes. "*Anyway,* I just want you to be able to follow through on all those promises you made earlier. I'm ready for you to kiss every inch of my body."

"And I can't read minds. That just shows how connected I am to you. I know you even though I just met you." He pulled her into his arms and kissed her.

His lips caressed hers with a slowly building passion—one that threatened to grow so large that it would consume them both where they stood. The initial press of his lips against hers pushed until she yielded and then pushed some more. The kiss became a mixture of tongues and teeth and hands, and soon she didn't know where he stopped and she began. Her tongue became his. He owned it and made it follow his lead. When her tongue dared to go off on its own or tried to move back into her mouth, he gently nipped her bottom lip and sufficiently scolded so she followed his lead again.

Their mouths performed this dance for several minutes, even though it felt like forever. When he finally pulled away, she felt drunk with him. The scent of nutmeg, summer rain and desire mixed in with the sand and salt water of the Atlantic Ocean.

"We should head back to my place. I have a feeling if we stay here they may arrest us for public indecency."

"Ya think?" she asked sarcastically.

He kissed her again and gave her a playful smack on the behind. "I know. So come on. I have promises to keep." He winked.

When they finally got to his loft, she could barely contain herself. She'd never felt so much need, ever.

They started taking off their clothing as soon as the door shut behind them, and they landed on the sectional sofa before reaching the bedroom. Darius set her on the sectional sofa and kneeled in front of her. He spread her legs and then gently stroked her with his long, sure fingers while he leaned forward and took her nipple in his mouth. He sucked on her nipples, one after the other, making a feast of her breasts. He stroked his fingers in and out of her, teasing her slick folds until she was almost at the peak of orgasm, and then he removed his fingers and her breast fell out of his mouth with a pop.

He then began to lick and nip and tease and caress her belly and neck and legs and thighs—every inch of her body—just like he'd promised. He explored her body at his leisure, and then he began to suck her nipples and stroke her sex with his fingers again until she was just on the edge. Then he stopped.

She tried to clutch his hands with her thighs. She tried to clasp his head to her breasts with her hands. She tried everything she could to keep him working long enough for her to finally have release. But he always stopped just shy of her having a screaming orgasm.

She thought she was going to go mad with need and called him everything but a child of God in her mind. But she didn't dare voice a word of it for fear that he would never finish what he started. She needed him to bring the fire he was building in her to its full, brilliant blaze.

But he seemed to need something from her, too.

What? What does he need?

She thought about their conversation on the Coney Island beach, and a lightbulb went off.

"I need you, Darius. Please. I need you." She clutched the back of his head. "No one has ever made me feel like this. *Ever.* And no one ever will. You've marked me, Darius, and I'm yours forever."

She could have sworn she heard a growl escape from his mouth, and his sucking intensified to an almost painful degree. His fingers worked her faster and faster. His thumb pressed against her clitoris, and the most mind-blowing orgasm she had ever experienced ripped through her and sent her into shuddering convulsions. Her eyes went halfway shut, and she barely noticed when he pulled her off the sofa, positioned her in front of it and grabbed a condom out of his pocket. She did notice the sound of ripping plastic and the way it felt when he entered her all the way to the hilt.

She let out a sharp cry and moved her hips back toward him. She felt impossibly full from this position, and as impossible as it seemed, she still wanted more. She pushed back farther and farther, meeting him thrust for thrust.

He held on to her hips with one hand while he used his other hand to trail her body. His hand moved across her backside with a feather-soft touch, and then he smacked her bottom. The sting of the smack jolted her, and it was followed by another feather-soft caress. Each thrust of his hips seemed to be punctuated with a caress and a smack.

In. Out. Caress. Smack. In. Out. Caress. Smack. It was over and over until she felt herself shaking with another incredible orgasm.

"Darius."

"That's right, Karen. Say my name, baby. Tell me, baby. You know what I want to hear."

"Oh. Shit."

He gave her bottom another smack. "That's not what I want to hear, baby."

Another miniature orgasm ripped through her, and she marveled that she'd had no idea she was multiorgasmic. No one had ever brought this out of her before. No one had ever known her this deeply, this completely. And no one had ever controlled, hell, owned her body in such an intimate and powerful way.

"It's yours!" She didn't care who knew it. She would have screamed it from the rooftop if it meant he would continue to love her like this. "It's yours, Darius! Yours."

His stroke became faster and more deliberate. "That's what I wanted to hear, baby. That's exactly what I needed to hear."

I think I love you, she whispered in her own head, afraid to say the words out loud and wondering how long she'd be able to hold back from making the declaration aloud.

He leaned forward and nibbled on her neck, all the while stroking in and out of her like a well-oiled piston. He let out a stuttered breath. "And I know you love me, Karen, even if you don't want to say it. I know it because

I love you, too." He nipped her earlobe and continued stroking her until she came yet again and he came with her.

He picked her up and carried her to the bedroom.

She sighed and pressed her head to his muscular chest. "One of these days I'm going to figure out how you do that. How do you always seem to know exactly what I'm thinking?"

Cullen stared at the documents on his desk. He had Karen's signature exactly where he needed it. When Darius saw these documents, their little romance would be over. He only had a few more pieces of the puzzle to put in place before it all fell down around the two lovebirds. There would be no happy ending this time around. He had lots of plans for Darius, and he wasn't about to let that little bitch ruin them.

He picked up his phone and dialed another pretty much useless bitch to see if she had held up her end of the bargain.

"Hello."

"Hello? Who is this?"

"This is Cullen. I need to know if we're all set. Did you make sure that special delivery is going to be made to Darius's place tonight? You gave them his keys, didn't you?"

"Damn it, Cullen! I told you I'd do it. You just better make sure it doesn't come back to me, or I will tell that it was you who put me up to this."

"Don't threaten me! Do you really want Darius to know that his own family member is the reason behind him having to come home and bury his cousin? You really need to be more careful whom you end up owing money to. One would think that a gambling pro such as you would have learned that lesson by now. I bailed you out and paid your debts. I expect results."

The other end of the line was silent for a minute. "I said it's handled. Don't worry. I want him focused on his career again, too. And I want him to get the hell out of Brooklyn. I haven't been able to do anything with him lurking around, so don't worry. It's handled, and I'll pay you your damn money back as soon as I can get him out of town and hit big." She hung up the phone.

Cullen thought about calling her back, but he knew she would come through because frankly she had no other choice.

Chapter 15

Roaming hands woke him up from his sleep, and he smiled at the thought that Karen clearly was up for some more loving. They had made love once again before they dropped off to sleep fully sated and satisfied. He rolled over and pulled her close, letting his hands caress her body. When his hands touched her breasts, he knew something was wrong. Karen's breasts were soft and had a texture and feel to them that he could only describe as *real*. These breasts were hard and felt like silicone.

"What the hell?" He jumped out of the bed and switched on the light. A blonde white woman and a black woman were in the king-size bed with him and Karen, and they were both nude.

They looked familiar, but he couldn't place them at all.

Karen sat up rubbing her eyes and looking about as

perplexed as he felt. She stared at the two naked women, and her eyes suddenly popped wide open.

The two women were lounging on his bed.

Karen jumped out of the bed, pulling the comforter with her and wrapping it around her. She shot him an accusing look, and he felt as if someone had taken a knife to his soul.

"Hey, D-Roc, when you invited us to join you and your little plaything, we didn't know you would get started without us, sugar." The blonde crawled out of the bed and over to him. She inched up his leg, and he shook her off.

"So, we decided we'd just join in. Thanks for the keys. We let ourselves in just like you told us. And we even remembered the alarm code this time, although you didn't have it on." The black woman stretched out on the bed and spread her legs.

"I didn't give you keys to my place! I don't even know who the hell you are. But I know one thing. You're going to get the hell out of here. Now! Get the hell out!" Darius didn't know if he should call the cops, drag them out himself or what.

Karen was glaring at him. "They're your *fans* from the restaurant the other night, Darius! Don't you remember giving them your autograph and taking a picture with them?" Her voice sounded eerily calm, too damn calm.

He had a feeling he was losing her before he ever really had her. He couldn't go out like that. He just couldn't.

"See there, sugar, your plaything remembers us even though you're playing hard to get." The blonde started inching up his leg again, and he shook her off once more.

He walked over to Karen.

The black one gave him a taunting look. "He wasn't playing hard to get when he gave us his phone number with his autograph. He wasn't playing hard to get when we had a threesome that very night. Oh, he played a little hard to get in the club the next night." She stared Karen in the eye. "But he didn't seem to be playing hard to get when he invited us over for a foursome with his plaything."

Karen's mouth fell open, and she backed away from him, shaking her head. "I trusted you." Her lip quivered, and his heart broke in two. Her eyes narrowed, and she lifted her chin slightly. He could tell that she was physically shoring up her defenses.

Was this someone's idea of a joke? If so, it wasn't funny to him. Someone was screwing with his life, and he didn't find anything funny about it.

The hurt in Karen's voice and in her eyes felt like a thousand tiny cuts on his most vital organs. It felt like someone had ripped his soul from his body and burned it.

Karen was gritting her teeth together so tightly that she was almost afraid they would crack under the strain. It was all she could do not to break down crying right there, and that was the last thing she wanted to do. Those hoochie mamas weren't worth the tears, but Darius… Darius was supposed to be her soul mate. How could she have gotten it so wrong? And how could she have let him get her so open that she forgot to guard her heart?

She felt a lump growing in her chest, and soon she

could feel it in her gut and throat. The only reason Darius was able to get her to open up to him so quickly and so completely was because he was the other half of her. She knew that, and she didn't doubt that. Unfortunately, that knowledge made his betrayal all the more heartbreaking. He was the only man who had the power to hurt her like this, and he was the one man who was never supposed to…

She took another deep breath, trying to calm herself and beat back the pain. It wasn't working, and she was really scared that she might lose it in front of them. She couldn't do that. She had to keep it together. She looked at Darius, even though it hurt to do so. He seemed like he was shocked. But she reminded herself that he was an actor. He could probably act shocked as easily as he could act like he was a good guy.

"Karen, these tramps are lying. I would never do that to you. I would never disrespect you like that." He reached for her, and she moved out of his grasp.

She couldn't let him touch her—not yet, not until she figured out what was really going on. She wanted to believe that he wouldn't play her like this. But these were the same women from the restaurant, the same women she saw in the club the other night. She wanted to believe Darius, but could she really?

"Oh, now we're lying, huh, sugar? You weren't calling us liars Tuesday night." The blonde stood up, shaking her big teased-out hair.

"No. Tuesday night he wanted to spank it, didn't you, daddy?" The black one got up and stood by the blonde, who bent over and shook her behind. The black one slapped the blonde on the behind.

"Ooooo, it's yours, daddy." Both women started giggling.

A sharp pain darted through Karen's heart. The memory of the playful spanking Darius gave her earlier flashed in her mind. Karen took a calming breath and then another. She turned from the women and glared at Darius. Clearly the man liked to get his spank on with all kinds of women. She shook her head and took another breath. It hurt. It hurt to breathe. It hurt to stand there and feel anything at all. She had to get out of there. Whether she did it with dignity or not was another question altogether. She cut Darius what she hoped was an evil look. She had to get out of there. When she realized that they had disrobed in the living room and not the bedroom, she pulled herself together and left the room.

It was hard to walk and hold on to the comforter at the same time, but she managed until she heard Darius behind her. Why didn't he just stay back there with the floozies? She sped up her walk and then took off into a run. She just didn't want to be around him anymore. She wasn't sure she'd be able to hold it all in.

Darius ran after her because he knew what she was thinking, especially after the way they had just made love. He'd gotten a little freaky and tapped her bottom during their lovemaking. He knew that was probably the nail in the coffin for her, the ultimate proof.

She was trying to run with the comforter wrapped around her, and he was afraid she might hurt herself. She was already hurting enough. She was doing a great job of holding it in and keeping her poise, but he could feel her hurt in his soul. She didn't need to add physical injuries to the mix.

He felt like his entire world was falling down around him. He barely remembered signing autographs for those women, and he darn sure never had a threesome with them. He never gave them keys to his place or his security code either.

Only two other people had keys to his place and the code to his security system: his aunt and his grand-mother. He knew that neither of them would give these tramps the time of day, let alone his security code and the keys to his place. So how the hell did they get in there? And how did they make it past the doorman? Heads were going to roll once he figured everything out. That was for sure.

He caught up to Karen just as her feet got tangled in the comforter and she started to fall. All he could see was the pointed corner of his chrome dining table in front of her as he reached out and grabbed her. He pulled her to him and held her tight.

He didn't even want to think about what would have happened if she had hit her head on the corner of that table. It could have killed her!

He was getting rid of the damn thing as soon as possible.

"Let go of me, Darius. Let go of me!" She pushed him away as hard as she could. But he continued to hold her tight.

She pounded on him with her fists until she was spent. But he refused to let her go. He just couldn't let her go.

She dropped her head onto his chest, and he could

feel her holding everything in. It broke his heart. If he were stronger, he'd just let her go. But he couldn't.

The two tramps had gotten dressed and walked out of the bedroom.

"I guess the party is really over, huh, sugar? Oh, well…you win some, you lose some." The blonde winked at him.

"You just lost one!" The black one said with a sneer. "See ya, sucker." She threw what looked like a copy of his keys at him. "Oh, and if you really don't want us coming back around you should change the security code you gave us and let Sam the doorman know." She smirked.

He felt Karen's body jolt in his arms, and she took a deep breath. He continued to hold her tight.

"You two skanks better hope and pray I never see you again. Because I swear…" If he wasn't literally trying to hold on to Karen, he didn't trust what he would have done to those women.

His grandmother raised him not to hit women, and he would never dream of doing so. But those lying tramps brought out harsh feelings in him.

"Whatever, sucker!" the black one shouted.

"Toodles, sugar." The blonde smiled and winked again. And they left, slamming the door behind them.

"Those women were lying, Karen. You've gotta believe me." He rubbed her back.

She looked up at him and stared at him for several minutes. He hoped like hell she was trying to decide if she could believe him. He watched her struggle. He felt like he could feel her inner turmoil. When the resigned expression covered her face and she blinked back the wetness that started to pool in her eyes, he knew she had made her decision.

"Let me go, Darius. I need to get dressed and get out of here. I can't do this now. I can't."

He let her go. Their clothes were all over the loft from the door to the leather sectional. He got dressed and she got dressed. He dreaded where he knew things were going.

How did he find his soul mate, fall in love and lose her in less than a week? That had to be some all-time record.

Once she was fully dressed, she went to the door. He ran after her and grabbed her arm. "I'll take you home, Karen. It's late. Please…just let me take you home." He needed more time with her. He needed to be able to convince her that this was all a setup.

"I don't want to be around you right now, Darius." She wouldn't even look at him.

It wasn't right.

"I just need to be sure you make it home safe. It would kill me if something happened to you."

She glared at him then.

He didn't see hatred in her eyes. No, hatred he probably could have dealt with. What he saw was such a complete and total lack of trust and overwhelming disappointment. It shattered him just to know what little faith she had in him.

"Fine. You want to take me home? Fine. The sooner I get away from you the better."

He followed her out and prayed for some kind of divine intervention. He had to find a way to prove to her that he'd been set up. Because he just could *not* lose her.

She looked out the window the entire ride from his place to hers and didn't say a word. He begged and pleaded and tried his best to convince her that he didn't do the things those women said. But she refused to respond.

As soon as they pulled up to her building, she opened the door. Before she got out, she turned to him. Her stare was ice-cold, and the chill in her voice froze him out so thoroughly and completely that he felt it all around his heart. "If you have any decency in you at all, which I highly doubt you do, you would not come around my center or me ever again. Just please stay away from me, Darius. I don't ever want to see you again."

She calmly closed the car door and walked away. He thought about following her but decided that she needed time. He needed to go and see one of the two people who had spare keys to his place and knew his security codes. Only his grandmother and his aunt had access to that information for emergency purposes. And he knew his grandmother didn't have a thing to do with what just went down. That meant Janice had a lot of explaining to do.

Karen trudged the stairs to her apartment as if she were a zombie. So many thoughts were fighting for time in her head. Everything was scrambled as she tried to process all that had happened to her since getting the journal three weeks ago and meeting Darius this week.

It must have all been some kind of sick joke. But

how? And why? Why would someone purposely make her believe she'd found her soul mate only to have him turn out to be her absolute worst nightmare?

The tears she had taken such care at holding back when she was at Darius's place had started to fall, and the wetness on her face angered her to no end. The fact that she was actually shedding tears over this man that she'd known barely a week disgusted her.

And her heart was broken. That was the worst of it—the worst part of it all.

She walked up to her door and found Saul sitting in the doorway on the floor.

She frowned. He was the last person she wanted to see at that moment. Hadn't she just gone on and on earlier today about Darius being *the one*. And Saul had said he hoped Darius didn't play her.

That was the thing that made her want to ball up like a baby—the fact that she knew deep in her heart that the only way Darius could have hurt her the way he did was if she had truly believed he was the other part of her soul. And that was what hurt most of all.

Saul jumped up when she approached the door. "Oh, Queen, it's you. You startled me."

"Well, you are in my doorway, aren't you? What do you want, anyway?"

Saul stood up with the same big, black duffel bag he had from college on his shoulder. Oddly, she marveled how he always managed to travel so light. It was the last thing that should have been taking space in her mind, but there it was. Maybe she was going crazy after all?

"I was hoping that you'd take pity on an old friend who just got back into town and hasn't found a place yet. You know how strained things are with my peoples. And I didn't want to stir up hope in any of the exes. So, although I wasn't expecting you to be all in love when I got here, I remember your sofa was really comfortable. I hope your *man* won't mind if I crash at your place tonight." He gave her a hopeful look and then concern crossed his face.

"Forgive me for saying this, but you look horrible, Queen. What the hell happened? Better yet, where the hell is he? I'll find him and kick his ass." He dropped his duffel bag and wrapped her in his arms.

She couldn't hold it in any longer. She couldn't be strong any longer. Her heart was broken, and she couldn't keep pretending that it wasn't. She started crying, stilted sniffles at first and then full-on sobs. Once she got started, she didn't think she would be able to stop.

And there it was, the breakdown, the expected response for everything she had just gone through. Maybe she wasn't crazy after all? Maybe she was just incredibly unlucky?

Saul shushed her and held her and promised to make everything better. Somehow he got her keys and managed to get the two of them into her apartment and got her settled on the couch while he made some tea.

Through it all, she sobbed and told him everything that had happened that night just before her life had gone to hell. He listened like a good friend: with the proper amount of outrage and disdain. He wasn't her mother or Amina or any of her girlfriends, but he was there, and he wasn't a bad substitute.

When she finally finished crying, he just held her.

Chapter 16

Darius called in the troops, and his entourage was en route, meeting him at his grandmother's place. He didn't think he would need them to question his aunt, but something in his gut told him he would need them before the night was over. Three of the guys were his bodyguards and had been former cops. Some of the others were on his payroll for other things. But some of the men who made a career of hanging out with him were just his ride-or-die homeboys.

If nothing else, seeing a large group of black men who clearly had his back was an intimidation factor. People seemed to talk more when they were scared something was about to jump off. If he needed them tonight once he found out more about those tramps who set him up, they'd be there.

When Darius pulled up to his grandmother's house, he noticed a strange car in the driveway. He pulled up just in time to see the blonde and the sister walking to the car, laughing and counting money.

His heart dropped because he didn't want to think that his aunt Janice had been the one to play him like that. But it had to have been her. The proof was getting in the car and driving away. He called his boys, and luckily they were right around the corner. He gave them the description of the car, and they agreed to follow them and catch them. One way or the other, he was going to get answers tonight. If his aunt wouldn't talk to him then he'd make those tramps talk and give up why his aunt had played him like that.

Once his cell phone rang and his boys told him they had the women in sight and would have them back at his grandmother's place shortly, he got out of his car and went inside the house to confront Janice.

When he got inside, he was surprised to see his grandmother up and in the kitchen. It was close to midnight. She was hardly ever up that late, and yet there she was in the kitchen with a bottle of Johnny Walker Black and a glass. He noticed two other glasses at the table with lipstick prints on them.

Had Janice just been in there toasting to their success with those women? Had they woken his grandmother up and left this mess for her to clean up?

"Grandma, what're you doing up at this hour of the night? Where's Janice?"

She jumped up, clutched her chest and knocked over her chair as well as the bottle of Johnny Walker Black. "My goodness, Darius. What are you doing sneaking up on your poor old grandmother at this hour of the night? You almost gave me a heart attack." She patted her chest, and her eyes darted around. "When did you get here?"

"I just got here a couple of seconds ago. I need to talk to aunt Janice."

His grandmother walked over and gave him a hug. "It's good to see you, son. Janice isn't here, though. She's out with some ole man she met online in some chat room or some such foolishness. I told her she shouldn't be just meeting men God knows where. She needs to come to church. But you know how Janice is. Her head is as hard as a rock—always has been. What do you want to talk to your aunt about? Is it Frankie? You look horrible. Are you still stressing about Frankie? Lord, I told that boy to stay out of them streets. Bad people in them streets waiting to catch you slipping." His grandmother was fluttering around and talking a mile a minute. She seemed nervous.

Confused, he shook his head and sat down. "Are you sure Janice isn't here, Grandma?"

Janice had to be there.

Because if she wasn't there, that would mean one of two things: either she got his grandmother to wait up for the women when the deed was done or...

No! Please, God, no!

He covered his face with his hands and shook his head.

His grandmother picked up her chair and cleared off the table, removing the three glasses and the bottle of Johnny Walker Black. She grabbed some paper towels and a wet dishrag to clean up the mess. He narrowed his eyes on her as she flittered around the kitchen.

"You want some tea or something? You look like

you've had a rough night. You need to talk about it? I'm not Janice, but I could listen. You used to tell me everything when you were a little boy. Would you like some pie? I think I still have some sweet potato pie left. I can cut you a slice." She started to get up.

"That's okay, Grandma. I was really only stopping by to see Janice. I'm having girl trouble, and I thought she might be able to offer some insight into the female mind."

His insides felt raw, gutted. For the second time since his cousin's funeral, he actually felt like he wanted to cry, not just cry, howl at the injustice of it all.

Janice betraying him would have been one thing, and he would have expected it.

But this?

This was just too much to take. And it cut him so deep that he almost thought something was physically wrong with him.

Can a person die from this kind of betrayal?

Because he felt like a part of him was surely dying, even if there wasn't any telltale physical signs. Something in him had died.

He wanted to shout, scream, rage, all of that.

He wanted to sob and ask her why, how?

How could she of all people do this to him?

"Girl trouble? What happened? You can tell me all about it." She seemed like she really cared, like she really wanted to help make it all better.

It was all he could do not to snarl. He took a deep breath and told her everything that happened that night from the time the two tramps showed up to him coming to confront Janice.

She listened intently and shook her head. "Now, I know you don't think Janice had anything to do with sending naked women to your place, do you? I know y'all have had your differences over the years, but she wouldn't do you like that. You're family. We're all that's left of our family."

She paused, and he found it hard to look at her with a straight face, especially when she started spouting off about family.

"Now this girl you claim to have lost. Maybe that was for the better. With your kind of jet-set lifestyle, it's hard to find a girl who can really deal with all that. And if she ran at the first sign of trouble—even after you tried to explain things to her—well, maybe she isn't the girl for you." She paused and gave him one of her encouraging smiles—one of the smiles that used to make him think he could take on the world and win because people loved him and had his back.

He could feel the anger building in his gut about to blast forth. He bit down and squashed it. No matter what, she was still his grandmother.

"I know it hurts. But sometimes you just have to let things go. You need to just pour yourself into your work right now—maybe go back to Hollywood and get your creative juices flowing. Wasn't there some hot, new producer in California you said you wanted to work with? Or maybe some new movies you could try out for. In your business, you've got to strike while you're hot, and you're smoking now, son! I'm *so* proud of you. Just forget about that girl, and think about what's important right now." She rambled on, and he just looked at her.

He knew it then for sure. In his gut, he knew that his grandmother had set him up.

"Grandma, only two people knew my security codes, had keys to my place and could have set me up like this. You and Janice."

"Only me and Janice? What about your friends and your employees? None of them have keys to your place? One of them could have done it. You know folks are backstabbers. Smile in your face and all the while they wanna take your place. Maybe one of your boys wanted to be there to pick up the pieces when you lost your girl? It happens all the time."

"My boys don't have keys to my place, Grandma. Only you and Janice." He stared at her.

She folded her hands on the table and fiddled with them for a moment before looking him dead in the eye. "Oh. I see. It must have been Janice, then."

His cell phone rang, and he excused himself from the kitchen to take the call. It was Rob, one of his bodyguards who used to be a cop. They had the girls, and it hadn't taken them long to get them to talk.

He listened to Rob tell him that the girls were tied to Cullen. And Cullen told them to approach him and show up at places where he'd be. His grandmother had provided the keys to his place and was responsible for paying them the second half of the money once the job was done.

He listened with half an ear and half a heart. He'd already known that his grandmother had betrayed him, and knowing that had already killed him inside. He thanked Rob and told them to stay outside with the girls until he called them, and he went back into the kitchen with his grandmother.

Numb.

He couldn't feel a thing. He didn't think he could feel any worse than he felt earlier tonight when he watched the woman he loved crumble, heartbroken, right in front of him.

But he'd been wrong.

Knowing that the woman who loved, raised and cared for him all these years was the reason behind Karen's broken heart made him feel one hundred times worse.

"Grandma, the guys are outside. See, I left out the part about having them meet me here. And I left out the part about me pulling up and seeing those low-life skanks leaving this house—the house I paid for—counting cash money as they laughed and got in their car. And I need to know if there is anything *you* want to say to me, your grandson—the man you claim to love like your own son. Is there anything you want to say to me, Grandma, before I bring them in here to tell their side of the story?"

His grandmother looked up at him with tears in her eyes. Where he normally would have gone to her immediately and tried to console her, all he could do now was sit there and watch her as she started sobbing.

"I'm sorry, Darius. I'm so sorry. I didn't want to hurt you, but the gambling came back and I was in so deep this time. They wanted their money, and they killed Frankie to send a message. If he had just stayed in school like you told him, they wouldn't have found him. But that boy never could stay off them streets. And Cullen helped me. He heard about the debt, and he paid it off for me, because those people were serious. They were almost as bad as the people who killed your mother. *Oh, Lord,* why did the gambling have to come back? I was too ashamed to tell you. I didn't want you to know this about me. I didn't want you to know that I was to blame. That's why I went to Cullen for help. Lord, I was so good for so many years. So many years after I lost my child, I cleaned up to take care of you and do right by her. Then Janice had Frankie so young and couldn't be a mother really. So I had him to focus on. But he grew up, and I didn't have nobody left. Janice just runs the street looking for men. I just needed something."

He wanted to scream, but nothing could come out.

His grandmother had a gambling problem so bad that people were willing to kill to get her to pay back her debt? His mother? His cousin? Dead because of her?

A gush of air came from his gut to his mouth. He opened his lips, but no sound came out. Now he understood why Karen could barely talk earlier that evening. He now knew what it felt like to be utterly and completely shattered.

He sat there for a few minutes, which seemed like hours, listening to her cry. Finally, he was able to speak. "You owed so much money that you got my mother and little cousin killed? You had to take money from my manager? And you had to set me up? Why? Why did you have to set me up? How could you do this?"

"I'm sick. I need help. I go to church, and I pray on it and I pray on it and I'm trying so hard. I want to stop. I didn't want you to know. I didn't want you to know that it was my fault Frankie was murdered. I was so ashamed. My grandbaby was killed because of me just like my oldest baby girl was murdered because of me. I didn't want to see you look at me like that. I didn't want anybody to know. I thought I could handle it and stop. I didn't want you and Janice to know that my gambling debts got Frankie killed. I didn't want you to hate me. I wanted to keep it a secret, and Cullen was going to tell...plus he had paid my debts. So I had to do what he said. I had to put the bugs in your house so he'd know when to send the girls. I had to give those women the keys and the security code. I had to pay the other half of their payment as part of my debt to him, the bastard. Oh...son...I didn't want to hurt you. And now that you know, I can try and help you get your girl back—"

"I don't want your help!" He stood up. "Clearly you and those tramps were in here toasting to a job well done. And you should pat yourself on the back, Grandma. Because if you wanted to see me broken, you did an excellent job!" He glared at her.

He took a deep breath and knew he had to leave before he said something that couldn't be taken back. She was still his grandmother, the woman who had raised him—even if he no longer recognized her. The weight of the situation was just too much.

"You say you need help? Okay, I'll pay for you to get the help you need, Grandma. You raised me. I guess I owe you for that. And I'll even continue to pay the bills here so that you and Janice can have a roof over your heads. But after today, I no longer have a grandmother." He then got up and left.

Cullen signed the letter and placed it in the envelope. He pursed his lips in contemplation. Things had certainly taken an unexpected turn.

The phone call from Darius's grandmother surprised him to say the least. He should have known that the old woman would eventually crack under pressure. He hadn't factored in Darius automatically going to blame his aunt.

Where's the trust in families these days?

He chuckled.

How was he supposed to know that Darius had only given those two women and no one else his keys and codes? He'd figured that at least his bodyguards would have had access and it would have taken Darius a little longer to figure out exactly how he got set up if he ever figured it out at all.

And now they had Peaches and Cream. He had grown rather fond of his recent playthings and would hate for anything to happen to them. But he wasn't about to stick around and wait for Darius to show up at his place with his band of merry roughnecks.

Sometimes you have to have collateral damage.

However, Cullen still had one ace to play. Darius hadn't won this round yet. Cullen would have given anything to see how crushed the little rapper was when he saw Karen's signature on those documents. The documents along with a note implying that she was in cahoots with Saul to murder D-Roc and a copy of the DVD of Saul shooting Shemar would crush the boy even more than him finding out that his grandmother had betrayed him. If only he could have been there when Darius figured that out!

Cullen laughed.

He was so glad he'd had the foresight to have someone

in the alley behind the studio to capture Shemar's murder for his continued viewing pleasure. Watching that cocky rapper get his over and over again made him feel all warm and tingly inside. The only thing better than that would be seeing the look on Darius's face when he got this package and Cullen's note, or when he showed up at that bitch's place and found Saul there. Too bad he couldn't stick around for any of it. If only there was time to have someone film it for him…

He turned to his manservant. "Get my lawyer and my accountant on the phone. I need the bulk of my finances moved to Swiss bank accounts yesterday! And my lawyer needs to be ready with a kick-ass criminal defense team just in case that idiot Saul forgets that snitches get stitches. I don't expect him to tell who hired him, but you never know." Cullen chuckled.

You win some and you lose some.

At the end of the day, it was all about how you played the game.

It wasn't even about Darius or his little bitch—not really. It was about winning the bigger game and coming out ahead of the family that had forsaken him a long time ago.

Divine might have won this round, but some of his cards were still out there waiting to be played. And even if she did win this round, there were many rounds to be played in the future.

Hell, he could play this game forever.

"Didn't I say get my damn lawyer on the phone? Use the cell phone, idiot! Let's get out of here before Darius shows up. Put this package outside in front of the door. Let's roll!"

* * *

When he and his boys ended up at Cullen's place with the women in tow, Darius almost thought they were going to have to break down the door to get in there and get some answers. It became clear that his grandmother had called Cullen after he left her house and warned him, because no one was there. After several minutes passed, it was apparent they weren't going to get an answer from the dark house.

"Hey, D-Roc, check this out. This has your name on it." Rob picked up a large envelope and opened it. "It's some papers and a DVD."

Darius ran his hand across his face and looked up toward the sky.

What now?

He let out a sigh.

"I have a DVD player in my SUV. We can see what's on this." Rob said. He turned to the women and then back to Darius. "Are we taking them with us?"

Darius frowned and shook his head.

He walked away from Cullen's house with the rest of the crew.

"What about us, sugar?" The blonde woman was standing on the steps with her hands on her hips.

"Your boys made us leave our damn car!" the black one yelled.

Darius turned and glared at them. His frustration level was beyond high. He'd really wanted to confront Cullen. And the fact that he wasn't going to be able to left him with very little patience for the floozies.

"What about you? You've been returned to Cullen. I suggest you call a cab or something. I really could care less. Just make sure you stay the hell away from me and mine."

He and Rob got into Rob's luxury SUV. Darius took out Cullen's note first and read it.

Darius,

Sorry I couldn't stick around and wait for you to show up. I hope that one day you realize everything I did for you and your career. I tried to keep that little gold-digging bitch from getting her claws into you. So I paid her off. I also did some digging into her past and the people around her. And I found video footage from the night Shemar was gunned down. Apparently someone was there documenting activity in that alley behind the studio where Shemar was murdered. The DVD cost me a lot, but I was curious to see who had taken down the great Shemar Sunyetta. Karen's love killed Shemar, and she inherited a lot of money. Tell me, do you think it was a coincidence that Saul showed up now when she had another hot rapper in her grasp? Please use your head. I have a feeling they were planning a similar demise for you. I bet if you went to her place now, you'd find them together. In this envelope, you will find a copy of the video and documents signed by Karen Williams that show she was willing to dump you for a measly $50,000.00. I have no way of knowing if she was going to keep her word and leave you alone. But I had to try. I hope that this evidence convinces you that I had your best interest at heart. If it doesn't? Well...more power

to you. You can't say I didn't try. Finally, do not
harm Peaches and Cream. They are innocent in
all of this. They just wanted to help me help you.
I guess no good deed goes unpunished.
Cullen Stamps

Darius let out a harsh huff and passed the note to Rob.
He didn't believe a single word of Cullen's note—not
after everything that went down. If Cullen really had
his best interests in mind then he would have come to
him like a man and not send two tramps to invade his
private space.

Darius pulled out the other documents in the envelope.
He looked at the papers with Karen's signature. They
were contracts, one stating that she would stop seeing
Darius, which was signed by Cullen and Karen, and
another to authorize the transfer of funds from Cullen's
account to the center's account.

Darius shook his head. That crap had to be fake or
forged, because he knew Karen wouldn't have done
anything like that.

But then he'd also known that his grandmother was
the one woman he could count on to have his back and
that she never would have betrayed him for anything in
the world. Could Karen turn out to be just as faithless
as his grandmother? He shook his head.

No.

He didn't believe it. He'd need more than Cullen's
letter and those bogus documents as proof.

A calm unlike anything he had ever felt came over
him. "Turn the DVD on."

Rob turned the DVD on, and they watched the

overhead flip-down monitor in silence. Even though the image was on such a small screen, the DVD showed clear as day Saul murdering Shemar.

"Damn." Rob let out a hiss of breath. "I know I don't have to tell you what you have to do with this DVD, man. It's evidence of a crime, and it should go to the police unless you want to be arrested as an accessory after the fact?"

Rob had been a cop before becoming Darius's head bodyguard. But Darius didn't need a moral compass on this one. He already knew the right thing to do.

"We're turning the DVD in to the police. Saul has to pay for what he's done." Darius's head was spinning, and he didn't know what to believe anymore. But he did know that he wasn't going to let that murderer continue to walk free around Karen or the youth at her center.

"And what if your girl Karen had something to do with it? What if she was trying to have you killed by Saul, as well, once she got you open enough to put her in your will? Would you be okay with it if this DVD went to the police and it took her down, too?"

"If she was involved in any way with Saul taking that man's life then she isn't the woman I thought I loved. So, yes, I'd be fine with her paying the price for her crime." He let out a sharp breath, and he realized he meant every word he'd just said. "Let's stop by Karen's place first."

Even though he had no idea how he would feel if it were true, he wanted to see if Saul was there.

Chapter 17

The harsh knocking on the door jolted Karen from the few minutes of sleep she had managed to get. She had left Saul on the sofa an hour ago. They both agreed that she should have one of her staff members open up the center in the morning because for the first time since she staffed the center she was in no shape mentally to be there.

She had just placed her head on her pillow and had finally been able to doze off when someone decided to bang on her door like the Gestapo. She got out of bed and walked out into the living room just in time to see Saul opening the door.

Darius barged in followed by seven more men. They looked like the men who had been at the club with them the other night. But she couldn't tell. Two of the men grabbed Saul and started frisking him.

"He's clean," the biggest and burliest one of the

bunch said. But they still held on to Saul and didn't let him go.

The entire time Darius was just staring at her. She started to feel way underdressed in the lavender nightshirt that came just under her behind and had the slogan, "This Is What A Feminist Looks Like" in purple letters. She wrapped her arms around herself.

"What's going on here, Darius? Why are you here? Why are you doing this? Haven't you done enough? I told you to stay away from me. It's over between us. I guess I'll see you next lifetime." She rolled her eyes. "But do me a favor, stay the hell away from me then, too. Asshole!"

He just stared at her and then looked over at his boys holding Saul. He noticed Saul was shirtless with just his pants on at about the same time she did. He turned back to her with all kinds of accusations in his eyes, and she thought he had some nerve given the black and white Bobbsey twins who had ruined their evening.

"Go put on a robe or put on some clothes, Karen." Darius gave the order like he paid rent there or like he thought somebody was going to actually listen to him.

He had the wrong somebody as far as she was concerned. She knew that much. She folded her arms across her chest, tilted her head and glared at him.

"I'm not doing anything. This is my apartment, Darius. You can't just come busting in here making demands. In fact, I think you need to take your thugs and leave."

Darius narrowed his eyes and spoke between clenched teeth. "Go and put on a robe or some clothes now, or I will take you back there and help you with that, Karen."

She noticed that all eyes in the room were now firmly on her.

One of the men took his eyes off her and noticed Saul's duffel bag by the sofa. He went right over and started looking through it. He pulled out a gun with his handkerchief and held it up for everyone to see.

"I do a lot of traveling. I need protection. And unless y'all are the police and are about to read a brother his rights then y'all need to just step off." Saul struggled to break free from the men holding him.

The sight of the gun made her eyes bulge. What the hell was Saul doing with a gun in her house? The man kept looking through the bag and came up with several wads of cash rolled up in rubber bands. He put everything back in the bag and put the bag to the side all the while continuing to stand by it.

Darius was barely paying attention to the gun or the cash apparently. Because while she stood there shocked with her mouth hanging open, she heard, "Karen, I'm gonna tell you one more time to put some damn clothes on."

Her head snapped up, and she looked him in the eye. Something was very wrong here, and for the life of her, she didn't know what. But she did know she wasn't going to test fate to see if Darius was crazy enough to make good on his threat to take her back in her bedroom and make her get dressed.

He didn't seem exactly like himself—whoever the hell that was.

She realized she'd **never really** known him at all.

But she wasn't foolish enough to try and find out at that particular moment.

She went back to her bedroom and quickly threw on a bra and a T-shirt and some jeans. When she came back out, she saw that Darius was putting a disk into her DVD player.

"Are you happy now? I'm dressed. Can you please tell me why the hell you're here? I told you I didn't want to see you again."

"Just watch this DVD, and tell me if you knew anything about this," Darius said in a no-nonsense voice that grated her nerves.

She walked over to her little twenty-seven-inch television, and what she saw literally brought her to her knees. She dropped where she stood, and the tears started immediately. There, for all to see, was Saul waiting in the same alley where Shemar's body had been found shot to death. Saul murdered Shemar and walked away like it was nothing.

"Nooooo!" She heard the loud cry that didn't even sound human to her own ears and realized that it was her own voice.

"No. No. No. No," she whispered as she sobbed.

Shemar was her best friend. They went back all the way to when she was in the first grade and a new kid in the neighborhood. Shemar had been her protector and her biggest advocate. He always had her back.

She stood up and ran over to Saul.

She went wild, striking him with her fists, hitting him with all the pain inside of her. She couldn't believe that she was the one who'd brought that monster into their lives.

How could she ever face Amina again?

"Queen, you know me. Think about it. It's clear that I'm being set up. That DVD must have been doctored. What reason would I have to kill Shemar? I knew how much he meant to you, Queen. I wouldn't hurt you like that. He is lying and trying to set me up!" Saul glared at Darius as he tried to pull away from her blows, but he couldn't move because Darius's men still held him.

She felt someone come up behind her and pull her away. She struggled, wanting to hurt someone as much as she was hurting at the moment.

"Look, I don't know what Cullen told you, but it wasn't me. I don't know where they found the look-alike, but it wasn't me." Saul glared at Darius and suddenly looked like the monster he was.

She wondered how she could have been so blind to it before now. Saul was a monster—a fake, lying, murdering monster.

"Who said anything about Cullen?" Darius slanted his eye at Saul.

Saul's face went blank for a moment, and then a panicked expression came across it. He opened his mouth and then closed it.

"We never said a word about Cullen. Why would you bring his name up? How do you know Cullen, Saul?" Darius was relentless.

Saul squinted his eyes angrily and gritted his teeth, but he refused to answer Darius.

"You might as well come clean. That's you on the DVD. The cops can easily authenticate it and prove it's not a fake. So you might as well tell us everything. Since you mentioned Cullen, you might want to start with how he knew you would be over here now. You working for Cullen?" Darius snapped.

"I don't have anything to say. And unless y'all are the police, y'all need to let me go and give me my shit. I don't have to tell you anything or admit to anything." Saul tried to pull away again.

"Rob, get this trash out of here and take him to your boys in blue along with that DVD and the gun. Who knows, it might even be the gun that shot Shemar. He looks stupid enough to keep it." Darius was holding her tight, and she was still trying to break away from him.

Saul tried to break away even more. He struggled with all his might, but the men held him fast.

"I hope that's enough to put him away." Darius frowned.

"The DVD might be enough, but a confession would be ideal. If the gun is the murder weapon, then he's as good as gone," one of the big guys holding Saul responded.

Saul started kicking his legs and really putting up a fight. "I'll deny it. I'll tell them y'all planted that gun. I'm not admitting to anything."

"Whose prints do you think they'll find on the gun? You might as well give it up," the big one said while shaking his head.

Karen's heart stopped. Saul's behavior told her everything she needed to know to confirm what she saw on the DVD with her own eyes.

Saul had murdered Shemar.

A raw and painful gasp escaped her throat, and her gut clutched.

"Get him out of here," Darius snapped.

The shock of everything left her raw.

The men left with Saul and his things in tow. Soon it was just her and Darius standing in her apartment. It was four o'clock in the morning. She was heartbroken and still reeling from everything that had just happened. She wanted him to leave her apartment so she could continue having her nervous breakdown in peace.

Was that too much to ask?

Darius locked the door and turned to her. He stared at her for several minutes, and her heart raced violently in her chest. She was in so much pain about Shemar's death, and the only thing she really wanted was for Darius to hold her until it didn't hurt so much anymore.

Was she crazy?

He walked over to her, picked her up into his arms and she lost it. She started sobbing all over again as he carried her to the sofa. He held her while she cried. She didn't know how much time had gone by. All she knew was the guilt was ripping through her chest and eating her alive.

"Shh. It's not your fault. It's not your fault." His words tried to soothe her back from the depths of despair.

Either his words had started to work or she was just spent, because the tears stopped. She glanced up at him and tried to move off his lap, but he held on to her.

"I didn't give those women keys to my place. I didn't have a threesome with them. I didn't even know them. My first and only time seeing them was the night they asked for autographs, and I didn't even remember them from that. I need you to believe me." He paused and looked at her intently.

"I need you to believe me because tonight Cullen

gave me documents with your signature on them that said you accepted money from him for the center as payment to stop seeing me. He gave me the DVD of Saul shooting Shemar because he wanted to plant the seed of doubt that you knew it was Saul all along and the two of you were in cahoots to make the same thing happen to me."

Her mouth dropped open in shock, and she shook her head.

Would this horrible night ever end?

"Everything inside of me screamed that you would never do that to me, Karen. *Everything.* I didn't want to believe that of you, so I kept faith in you—in *us.* And I came over here knowing in my heart that even if we found Saul over here, you wouldn't have done anything with him. I have faith in you. Do you have faith in me?"

His voice sounded so raw and emotional that it was breaking her heart all over again.

She suddenly didn't care if she was being a fool for trusting him. She just wanted him to stop hurting. "I have faith in you, Darius. Thank you for trying to help bring Shemar's murderer to justice."

"I need to tell you what happened." He went into everything that had happened that night after he dropped her off.

When he got to the part about his grandmother, the setup, the gambling and the murders of his family members, tears were rolling down his cheeks. She knew that Cullen Stamps was a snake, and everything Darius said about his role in the chain of events rang true. She felt horrible for not having more faith in Darius.

Even though she had never met the man, she could see Cullen hiring those tramps and blackmailing Darius's grandmother.

But the role his grandmother played in it all? Karen could tell by the tears falling down his strong, solemn face that his grandmother's betrayal cut him to the core.

She wrapped her arms around him and held him tight. It was her turn to comfort him now, her turn to try and take away some of his pain. She felt raw and numb all over again from his pain alone. The betrayal he had faced tonight was horrible and yet he came through for her and made sure that Saul and the DVD made it to the police station.

She ached for him, and her tears joined his as they cried together. When they stopped, he stared at her.

"I love you, Karen. I'm not perfect, and I know I'll probably make some mistakes along the way, but I need you to have faith in me. I need you to love me and stand by me the same way I love and will *always* stand by you."

She got up and straddled his lap. "I love you, too, Darius. I'm so sorry I didn't have more faith in us tonight. I'll do better if you give me a chance. I promise." She pressed her lips to his and kissed him with everything inside of her. She held him tight, and she never intended to let him go ever again.

She stood and took his hand, leading him into her bedroom. She slowly undressed him and led him over to the bed, making him sit on it while she knelt in front of him.

She kept her swollen eyes on him as she took him

in her mouth. He stared at her with all the love he had expressed earlier as she circled his manhood with her tongue and stroked him with everything inside of her.

She thought of the times he had pleasured her this way and renewed her efforts to bring him just as much pleasure as he had brought her. She clutched his behind, trying to bring as much of him as she could fit into her mouth. Just when she thought she couldn't fit any more Darius stood and his sex plopped from her lips. He lifted her up and started removing her clothing. Once she was nude, he grabbed his pants and put on protection. He got back on the bed and looked at her.

"I want you to ride me, baby. Make me feel it."

He didn't have to tell her twice. She straddled his lap and slowly enveloped his sex with hers. She pressed down and swiveled her hips and began to bounce—up, down, around and even sideways.

He reached up and teased her nipples, one in each hand. He pulled and tugged and twirled them until she could have sworn he was controlling the movement of her hips with the way he worked her nipples. Each pull and tug and twirl caused her to press and swivel and bounce.

She threw her head back and let out a soft hiss of air as a miniature orgasm pulsed through her. But her hiss turned into a holler once she realized that the small orgasm was just an opening act for the bigger one that ripped through her just seconds after the tiny one ebbed. She dropped her head and looked down at Darius again. He was still watching her intently as he maneuvered her nipples.

She leaned down, pressing her lips to his with a hard

and demanding kiss. His hands moved from her nipples to her behind. He clutched part of her hips and part of her behind, getting a good, firm grip on both sides. And he started to move her up and down his shaft, stroking her until the friction and the buildup was so intense she could barely contain herself. She started to buck wildly even though he was controlling her movements.

His hips started to lift up and met hers as he pressed her down. Soon he slammed her hips down and thrust his up and held them together tightly. The jumping contortions of his release triggered another orgasm in her, and they both reached completion together, panting and spent.

He got up and removed the protection, got back in the bed and wrapped her in his arms. The sunlight of a new day filtered through the blinds on her window as they drifted off to sleep still entwined.

They didn't wake up until sometime that evening. And when they did, the first thing Darius did was kiss Karen. He gave her a soft, lingering peck on the lips. He couldn't believe that he still had her. He hadn't lost her in spite of everything that happened.

She stifled a yawn. "Um, I can't believe we slept this late. I'm starving. What was that kiss for?"

"Because I love you. You know you're gonna be my wife, right?"

"I love you, too. And if that's you *asking* me to be your wife then the answer is yes even though I've only known you less than a week." She gave him that sassy little grin of hers that he loved.

"You've known me a lot longer than that, baby.

I'm your soul mate, and we're going to be together forever."

She smiled. "Oh, speaking of that, I had another dream, and I think this one was about the future, although it could have been the past. It looked really primitive. But anyway...I was a warrior princess, and you were this corrupt warrior prince and I was leading a resistance against the corrupt monarchy—"

He kissed her. "Enough about the past and the future. Let's focus on the here and now. Let's focus on making our slice of forever better than it ever has been or ever will be. If our souls dream about us in the future, I want them to be like, *damn!*" He laughed at his own joke.

She kissed him back. "I do like the sound of that." She deepened the kiss, and soon all either one of them could think about was the present and how they were never going to let each other go.

Epilogue

Sometime in the far future...

Kiona loved it when she got a chance to visit the relics auction. Ever since she was a kid, she had a zest for knowledge about history and a desire to collect things from days gone past. Books were her favorite.

Even though hardly anyone had read a bound book in decades and every piece of knowledge known to man was safely housed in heavily guarded computer data centers, she still had a collection of old books. Her favorite things to bid on in the relics auctions had to be books, followed closely by vintage clothing.

As she walked around the great hall and eyed the items up for auction, she also thought about how much she could afford to spend from her very limited budget. She worked part-time translating and transcribing ancient texts for the United Freedom of Knowledge Archive Federation. The work was flexible and allowed her to have the free time she needed for her true passion. Agitation!

She had to be ready to drop whatever she was doing whenever the text message for the next impromptu protest came through. The flash protest format started in the early part of the twenty-first century. But with new technology and so many causes in the world to protest, the old style of protest had taken on new dimensions. Once she received the electronic notification of when and where to be for any given protest, she could literally be there in minutes. Beam technology made it so that she could travel miles away, even to another country in the blink of an eye. What made things even better was the fact that Agitators could break out and beam away as soon as the police came to break up protests.

She'd found that employers didn't take kindly to employees beaming out of work to join a flash protest, even if they beamed right back within the space of an hour. So, she freelanced translating ancient texts part-time and spent the better part of her days and nights protesting injustices all across the globe.

Just as she was thinking it had been a rather slow day for flash protests, she eyed the most intriguing leather-bound book she had ever seen. It didn't have a title on the cover or the side binding, so she had no idea what the book was about, but she knew she had to have it.

She took a step closer to the book and was glad that it was a relic potential buyers could actually touch before the bidding started. There were some relics that they kept behind glass so that people could only look at them. She walked over and picked up the leather-bound book just as another hand reached for it.

The hand skimmed hers and sent tingles from her fingers to her chest. She clutched the book tighter and glanced up to see who had touched her. Most importantly, who had the nerve to want the book that she had to have!

He was tall, dark and devastating to say the least. His skin was the shade of the deepest, richest mahogany, and his eyes looked like orbs of obsidian. His jet-black hair held deep waves. And his build... His muscular build showed that he still found ways to work on his body during a time when most folks were content to beam everywhere instead of walk and sit around in front of their telecomps and computers all day. Yes, devastatingly handsome described him best. Too bad he reeked of Establishment. From his fancy suit to his state-of-the-art beamer and telecomp, he had Establishment written all over him.

"I'm bidding on this book. So you might as well find something else to bid on. There are lots of interesting relics here. This one is mine." She staked her claim and started to open the book to have a look inside.

Stunned, Dana stared at the woman in front of him. He was so captivated by her earthy beauty that he barely heard what she said. Her petite frame, creamy mocha skin and haunting gray eyes were speaking to him a lot more than the words coming out of her bow-shaped, very captivating mouth.

He shook his head. "Pardon, me, Ms.…" He waited for her to fill in her name, and she cut him a look that told him not to hold his breath.

"I see…well, my name is Dana Freedmen, and I collect relics such as these for the High Divine Church Federation."

"Establishment zealots." She smirked. "That makes me want this book all the more. I can't have it get into Establishment hands. It's bad enough access to knowledge is limited for the majority of the people of the world. I'll consider it my duty to liberate this book today."

What an infuriating woman! So why did he find himself so attracted to her? "Listen, Ms.…" He waited again for her to give him a name.

"The name is Kiona Graham. Not that it matters, because we don't run in the same circles, *obviously*."

"Well, Ms. Graham, I just wanted to make a deal with you." He pulled his telecomp from its side clamp and transmitted his contact information directly to her telecomp with the press of a button. "In the interest of being free with knowledge, I'll make you a deal. You can feel free to contact me after I outbid you on this book. I have deeper pockets, being Establishment and all…but I am willing to share."

She gave him an incredulous stare. "Don't expect me to do the same when I outbid you on this book, Dana. I have no plans on *ever* letting you see it." She sniffed. "What is that…smell? Did you not read the sign that this is a scent-free environment? There are people who are very sensitive to smells, and the use of scents, perfumes and the like has been banned in this country for years."

He sniffed. He smelled something all right, but it wasn't coming from him. It was coming from her. He couldn't pinpoint the scents. The only thing he knew was that she smelled really good, and the scent made him want her very much. It filled him with desire.

She sniffed and what might have passed for a smile if she were inclined to do so crossed her face. "It smells nice…but surely it's not worth the fine you would have to pay for wearing it in a public space." She shook her head.

He was just about to tell her that he wasn't wearing any scent and she clearly was, when the Divine High Priestess came walking over. He had hoped that his boss wouldn't come over and see him haggling with the annoying woman over the very item they had come to the auction to purchase. The Divine High Priestess had said it was imperative that they get this journal and that he translate it immediately. He really hoped that she hadn't heard their bickering.

The Divine High Priestess was a tall, dark-complexioned woman who wore her long, jet-black hair in beautiful long braids. She had an air of almost unearthly beauty, and at the same time, she seemed to embody all that was still good and pure about the planet Earth.

"Ah…I see you've found the relic, Dana. Good job, dear one." The Divine High Priestess looked at the journal, still unfortunately in Kiona's adorable hands.

"Yes, Divine one, I've found it and so has Ms. Kiona Graham. She has promised to outbid us on it."

The High Priestess smiled. "Well, then, we shall see who gets it, won't we. I'm going to take a seat. There's no need for you to look at the journal, Dana. That's the one we need."

The High Priestess walked away, and Dana smiled at Kiona. "May the best person win, then, Ms. Graham. Just remember you have my contact information if you ever want to come and look at the book. Good day." He walked off while he still could, cursing each and every step away from her. He had really wanted to stay and kiss her, taste her delectable lips until the end of time, forever if at all possible. But he had a feeling she would slay him where he stood if he tried to kiss her—and rightfully so. He just met the woman after all. So he walked away to join the High Priestess.

He took a seat by her and got ready for the bidding war to begin.

"She's not exactly what you were expecting, is she?" The High Priestess teased with a tilt of her lips.

"Who, Kiona? What do you mean, not what I expected? I certainly didn't expect to meet someone so passionate and infuriating who happened to want the very journal my boss told me I *must* acquire today."

"No. No. No. Dear one, I meant she's not what you expected to find when you found your soul mate." The High Priestess chuckled and stood up. "I trust you to get the journal and have the translating done by the end of the month. I think I'll go back to the Federation now."

* * *

Kiona watched the Divine High Priestess leave. She flipped through the book and got excited. She noticed the different handwritings in the book. It was some kind of journal or diary. But different people had written in it. It would be thrilling to begin translating it. Just looking at the dates alone she could tell that it would give her glimpses of real lives throughout time. The latest entry was in the early twenty-first century. What an amazing find! She had to get the book.

Just as she had that thought, her telecomp pulsed and she looked at the message. It was a message from her friend Cullen. He was thoroughly anti-Establishment, especially now that the Establishment was forcing religion down everyone's throat and he had set up some of the most world-renowned protests ever. She didn't have anything against religion, but she was against people not having the freedom to choose.

Cullen's text said that there was a flash protest against the containment efforts of the government in less than a minute right in front of the House of Nations.

She frowned and bit her lip in contemplation.

This was the kind of protest that came along once in a *long* while. The kind that Agitators like her bragged about being at for years to come.

She put the journal down. She took one more look at the journal and then at the tall, dark and devastating Dana before she beamed out. She really hoped that Dana guy got the book and had given her his right contact information. Because she fully intended to take him up on his generous offer!

She found herself thinking yet again how handsome he was. He was the kind of man a girl could easily see spending forever wrapped in his arms.

Easily?

Well maybe not easily but definitely forever…if she were looking for forever, that was.

The end…or because true love never dies and real soul mates can make it last forever, maybe it's just a new beginning.

* * * * *

L♥VE IN THE LIMELIGHT

Fantasy, Fame and Fortune...Hollywood-Style!

Book #1

By *New York Times* and *USA TODAY*
Bestselling Author Brenda Jackson

STAR OF HIS HEART

August 2010

Book #2

By A.C. Arthur

SING YOUR PLEASURE

September 2010

Book #3

By Ann Christopher

SEDUCED ON THE RED CARPET

October 2010

Book #4

By *Essence* Bestselling Author Adrianne Byrd

LOVERS PREMIERE

November 2010

Set in Hollywood's entertainment industry,
two unstoppable sisters and their two friends
find romance, glamour and dreams-come-true.

KIMANI™
ROMANCE

www.kimanipress.com
www.myspace.com/kimanipress

KPLITLSP

REQUEST YOUR FREE BOOKS!

2 FREE NOVELS
PLUS 2 *FREE GIFTS!*

KIMANI™
ROMANCE

Love's ultimate destination!

YES! Please send me 2 FREE Kimani™ Romance novels and my 2 FREE gifts (gifts are worth about $10). After receiving them, if I don't wish to receive any more books, I can return the shipping statement marked "cancel." If I don't cancel, I will receive 4 brand-new novels every month and be billed just $4.69 per book in the U.S. or $5.24 per book in Canada. That's a saving of over 20% off the cover price. It's quite a bargain! Shipping and handling is just 50¢ per book.* I understand that accepting the 2 free books and gifts places me under no obligation to buy anything. I can always return a shipment and cancel at any time. Even if I never buy another book from Kimani Press, the two free books and gifts are mine to keep forever.

168/368 XDN E7PZ

Name	(PLEASE PRINT)

Address	Apt. #

City	State/Prov.	Zip/Postal Code

Signature (if under 18, a parent or guardian must sign)

Mail to **The Reader Service:**

IN U.S.A.: P.O. Box 1867, Buffalo, NY 14240-1867
IN CANADA: P.O. Box 609, Fort Erie, Ontario L2A 5X3

Not valid for current subscribers to Kimani Romance books.

Want to try two free books from another line?
Call 1-800-873-8635 or visit www.morefreebooks.com.

* Terms and prices subject to change without notice. Prices do not include applicable taxes. N.Y. residents add applicable sales tax. Canadian residents will be charged applicable provincial taxes and GST. Offer not valid in Quebec. This offer is limited to one order per household. All orders subject to approval. Credit or debit balances in a customer's account(s) may be offset by any other outstanding balance owed by or to the customer. Please allow 4 to 6 weeks for delivery. Offer available while quantities last.

Your Privacy: Kimani Press is committed to protecting your privacy. Our Privacy Policy is available online at www.eHarlequin.com or upon request from the Reader Service. From time to time we make our lists of customers available to reputable third parties who may have a product or service of interest to you. If you would prefer we not share your name and address, please check here. ☐

Help us get it right—We strive for accurate, respectful and relevant communications. To clarify or modify your communication preferences, visit us at www.ReaderService.com/consumerschoice.

KROM10R

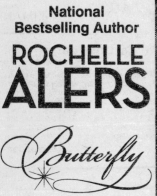